"Why don't you hire him?" Ricky motioned to Brody.

"Whoa, kid. I'm not looking for work. As a matter of fact, I'm on my way to Lubbock for a rodeo."

Another worthless cowboy.

"The wheelbarrow is out by the compost pile. Get busy." Once her son disappeared, Kat's gaze connected with Brody's. The man was too darn handsome. "Good luck with your rodeo." She spun, but he grasped her arm.

"I suppose I could help Ricky—"

"Oh, no, you don't. Don't go thinking I'm some helpless woman who needs a knight in shining armor to rescue her. I've been on my own a long time and I don't need a man to rescue me. Got that?"

"Yes, ma'am."

"Good."

Brody tipped his hat. "I'll leave you to your business."

Kat ignored the twinge of regret that Brody had backed off so quickly. Handsome cowboys were a waste of time. Kat ought to know—Ricky's father had used his good looks and charm to take her for a ride, then he'd tucked tail and run when she'd turned up pregnant.

Men. Who needed them?

Dear Reader,

The Bull Rider's Secret is the second book in my new series, Rodeo Rebels. Bull riders are considered the bad boys of rodeo. For most cowboys, it's the thrill of the eight-second ride that keeps them returning to the arena. Brody Murphy isn't like the average bull rider. He's not looking to best a bull—a good thing considering he stinks at the sport.

Brody Murphy rides bulls to keep his mind off the death of his young daughter. Not until he meets up with Katarina Sovo has Brody ever thought about putting down roots. Kat has her hands full with an unruly teenager and goals of her own that don't include becoming attached to a man who's around one day then gone the next.

I hope you enjoy watching the drama unfold as two fiercely independent people find in each other the courage to admit that what they really want is to be part of a family again.

If you missed the first book in my Rodeo Rebels series, *Rodeo Daddy* (April 2011), the book remains available through online retailers or can be ordered by your local bookstore. The third book in my Rodeo Rebels series hits store shelves December 2011. For more information on my books, please visit www.marinthomas.com or sign up for my newsletter at marin@marinthomas.com.

Until the next go-round!

Marin

The Bull Rider's Secret

MARIN THOMAS

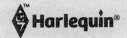

TORONTO NEW YORK LONDON
AMSTERDAM PARIS SYDNEY HAMBURG
STOCKHOLM ATHENS TOKYO MILAN MADRID
PRAGUE WARSAW BUDAPEST AUCKLAND

Recycling programs
for this product may
not exist in your area.

ISBN-13: 978-0-373-75368-0

THE BULL RIDER'S SECRET

ABOUT THE AUTHOR

Marin Thomas grew up in Janesville, Wisconsin. She attended the University of Arizona in Tucson on a Division I basketball scholarship. In 1986, she graduated with a B.A. in radio-television and married her college sweetheart in a five-minute ceremony in Las Vegas. Marin was inducted in May 2005 into the Janesville Sports Hall of Fame for her basketball accomplishments. Even though she now calls Chicago home, she's a living testament to the old adage "You can take the girl out of the small town, but you can't take the small town out of the girl." Marin's heart still lies in small-town life, which she loves to write about in her books.

Books by Marin Thomas

To my sister-in-law Denise

You're creative, talented, a good friend to many and always the life of the party. Thanks for reminding us not to take ourselves too seriously.

"I don't make monkeys, I just train 'em!"

Chapter One

The thunder of motorcycles roaring down Main Street threatened to deafen Brody Murphy as he used the pay phone outside the Silver Dollar Saloon in Bandera, Texas.

"Ma'am." Brody tipped his hat to a wannabe cowgirl who sashayed by, leaving a scented cloud of expensive perfume in her wake.

"What's that god-awful noise?" Brody's buddy, Drew Rawlins, shouted through the phone connection.

"The Hell's Angels are in town."

"Where are you?"

"I'm in Bandera."

"Bandera? You were supposed to be here—" meaning Drew's ranch, Dry Creek Acres "—three hours ago."

Brody ignored his friend's rant as he studied his choices for lunch across the street—Southern Comfort Bakery, Mi Pueblo, Busbee's Bar-B-Que and Bandera Saloon & Grill.

"Hey!" Drew snagged Brody's attention. "What are you doing in Bandera?"

Hell if Brody knew. He scanned the area, willing the

answer to pop up in front of him. His gaze landed on a flyer attached to the saloon's oversize red door.

Bandera, Texas
Cowboy Capital of the World
Wild Hog Explosion
Saturday March 20th at Mansfield Park

"Think I'll enter the Wild Hog Explosion." *Whatever the heck that was.*

"You're kidding, right?"

Maybe. Brody was down to twenty bucks in his wallet and half a tank of gas. Speaking of fuel, Brody gagged on fumes as a second pack of motorcycles drove past him.

"I offered you a job," Drew said.

Turning his back to the busy road, Brody rested his arm atop the pay phone. This wasn't the first time Drew suggested Brody quit the rodeo circuit and work for him as a ranch hand. Brody had been a ranch hand most of his adult life—punching cows in Montana where he'd been born and raised. Hell, he loved—make that *had* loved—working cattle and horses, wide-open spaces and the soul-searching loneliness of riding the proverbial range. Two years ago Brody had quit his job at the Black Stone Ranch and now he lived one day and one bull ride at a time.

There was a part of Brody that yearned to hang up his bull rope. He was tired. Lonely. Downright lost. But working for Drew would be like walking around all day with a red-hot poker stuck in his eye.

His buddy understood the demons chasing Brody. He

was the only person Brody had confided in about his past. Even so, Brody didn't care to witness the former bronc rider's happiness. Drew had retired from rodeo this past December after he'd scratched at the National Finals Rodeo in Vegas. He'd given up a world title for love and a chance to be a father to a son he hadn't known existed until recently.

Drew was happy. Brody was miserable. It would only be a matter of time before Brody's unhappiness ruined their friendship. If that wasn't enough to deter him from accepting a job at Dry Creek Acres, then taking charity from a friend was. Drew had offered the job, not because he needed help, but because he felt sorry for Brody.

"Thanks, but I've got a ride coming up," Brody lied.

"When are you gonna admit you aren't a bull rider?"

Never. "I'll be in touch."

"The job's yours anytime you want it."

"Thanks." Brody hung up and eyed the advertisement on the saloon door. *What the hell.* He'd head to Mansfield Park and check out the exploding pigs.

As Brody drove along the main drag, he did a double take at the horse hitched outside the Dairy Queen. Any town that allowed horses on the street was okay with him. He followed the signs to the park, mulling over his options. Bandera didn't have a rodeo until Memorial Day weekend, so there was no sense hanging around after today.

The past few months Brody had fought to maintain his enthusiasm for bull riding. Although he hadn't had much success in the sport, he'd basked in the thrill of the challenge and had enjoyed the camaraderie of his competitors. Then Drew had left the circuit and suddenly Brody's excitement for rodeo had spiraled downward. Quitting wasn't an option. His survival depended on never remaining in one place long enough for his past to catch up with him.

Yesterday he'd turned thirty-one, but he'd woken feeling fifty. He doubted his body could withstand the physical abuse of the sport much longer. In the two years he'd competed, he'd suffered eleven fractures. It wouldn't be long before the next broken bone refused to heal. Not a day went by that he didn't wish he had the courage to pull off this never-ending road to nowhere.

The gravel lot at Mansfield Park was crowded but Brody found a spot and parked. The smell of hickory and barbecue permeated the air and his stomach growled. Signs advertising a Pork Rib Cook-Off, Bicycle Rodeo, Piggy Pictures, Arts and Crafts, and Wild Hog Explosion were staked in the ground everywhere.

Brody observed a makeshift corral in the distance and made his way through the crowd. A banner proclaiming a five-hundred-dollar jackpot hung across the sign-up table—more than enough money to fill the gas tank, his belly and pay his next entry fee. There was just one problem—Brody needed a partner for the hog-catching contest.

He searched the crowd for loners who might be willing to team up with him. A teenager stood by himself near the boar pen. The kid was skinny, which hopefully meant he was quick on his feet. Brody would rather the teen chase the pig in circles than himself. "You lookin' for a partner, kid?"

The boy jumped inside his skin and stepped back. His blue eyes widened with apprehension.

"What's the matter?" With Brody's luck the teen was on the run from the law. "You in trouble?"

The kid's posture stiffened. "I'm not in any trouble."

"You here by yourself?"

"Yeah, so what?"

Nice chip on the ol' shoulder. Brody studied the kid. Olive-colored skin, black hair and startling blue eyes—a mix of Caucasian and Hispanic.

"I need a partner for the hog-catching contest. What do you say we team up? I'll give you a hundred bucks if we win."

The kid scoffed. "The jackpot's five hundred."

"How about one-fifty."

The boy stared at Brody's lace-up cowboy boots with a spur ridge on the heal. "You a rodeo cowboy?"

"Bull rider." Brody puffed out his chest.

"You any good?"

"Sometimes." *Mostly not.*

"How come you wanna catch a hog?"

"You sure do ask a lot of questions."

"Okay, I'll be your partner."

Brody motioned over his shoulder. "Let's sign in and pay the entry fee."

"I don't have any money."

"I'll cover you." Brody grinned. "If we win, you get a hundred-forty dollars."

"Gee, thanks." The kid trailed Brody, his hands shoved into the pockets of his sagging jeans.

"How old are you?" Brody asked when they reached the table.

"Thirteen."

The kid looked older—probably due to his lanky build and height. Brody wasn't a tall man. He stood five-feet-ten inches without his boots on and the boy almost looked him in the eye.

"You got a name?"

"Ricky Sovo."

"Brody Murphy." They shook hands, then signed a release form and paid the entry fee. They were told to wait until their names were called.

"You ever catch a hog before, Ricky?" Brody asked.

"Nope. You?"

"Nope."

They watched the pair inside the corral trip over themselves attempting to corner the pig. The buzzer rang and Ricky asked, "You got a plan on how we're gonna bag our hog?"

"You chase the bacon in circles until the oinker's too dizzy to run, then I toss the burlap sack over its head."

Ricky's jaw sagged. "Pigs don't get tired and we've only got three minutes to catch one."

"How fast can you run?"

"Real fast."

"Then my plan should work."

A half hour later their names were called. They entered the corral and Brody walked to the far side of the pen with the burlap bag. Ricky stood by the chute that held the female boar.

The announcer introduced Brody and Ricky, then the

gate opened, and the hog bolted for freedom. The teen hadn't joked when he'd bragged he could run—he was lightning fast. The crowd's cheers grew more enthusiastic, most folks forgetting Brody stood in the shadows.

He checked his watch—one minute had ticked off the clock. Ricky and the pig hadn't slowed down. Another minute passed and Brody moved to the center of the pen. Ricky continued to chase the hog counterclockwise. Drew waited for the right moment then stepped in the path of the pig, startling the animal. The boar stopped on a dime. Brody tossed the bag over its head and scooped up the oinker.

Caught off guard by Brody's actions, Ricky was unable to swerve out of the way and slammed into Brody. The two toppled to the ground, but Brody managed to hang on to the squealing burlap bag. The crowd erupted in applause.

"Good job, kid." Brody spit dirt from his mouth.

Chest heaving, Ricky smiled, revealing red-stained teeth.

"You split your lip." Brody handed the burlap bag to one of the event workers then helped Ricky off the ground. "Let's hope no one else succeeds and we don't have to share the pot." After they left the pen, Brody asked, "You still got all your teeth?"

Ricky stuck his finger into his mouth. "Yeah."

The winners wouldn't be announced until three o'clock, so Brody led the teen to a Porta Potti and grabbed a wad of toilet paper from inside. "Press this against your lip." He hoped the kid wouldn't get into trouble for competing in the event. "I guess your mom's going to be mad you got hurt today."

"My mom won't care."

"You hungry?"

Ricky's head bobbed up and down.

"Barbecue sounds good." Brody used his last ten dollars to purchase two food tickets. He and Ricky ordered pulled pork sandwiches and sodas then found an empty picnic table. The kid ate in silence, gulping his food despite his puffy lip.

"How come you aren't here today with your friends?" Most thirteen-year-old boys hung out in packs—that's the way Brody had grown up. When he'd met Kelly after he'd graduated from high school, he'd given up trolling with the guys.

"I don't have many friends," Ricky mumbled, his mouth full of barbecue.

"What do you do in your spare time?"

"Play video games."

"Does your mom work?"

"She shoes horses."

"A farrier, huh?"

Another nod.

"What about your father?"

"He doesn't live with us." Ricky's clipped answers suggested an unhappy teenager.

"My parents passed away a long time ago." Brody hadn't been close to his folks. "My mom thought she could never have kids and then at forty-nine years of age she got pregnant with me."

"That's old."

Forty-nine didn't seem all that old to Brody now that he'd entered his thirties. "I was a wild one growing up." He'd gotten into his share of trouble because his parents had been too old and too tired to ride herd over him. "We lived on a farm, but I hated plowing. I wanted to be a cowboy."

After Brody reached legal working age he no longer helped out in the fields, because his father hadn't been able to pay him. He'd punched cows for the local ranches to earn money to buy his first truck and pay for his clothes. After he'd graduated high school he'd signed on permanently with one of the ranches. He'd rarely given any thought to his aging parents until one day out of the blue his father had dropped dead of a heart attack. Brody had no love for farming, so his mother had sold the land and moved to Bozeman to live with her older brother and his wife. She'd died a year later—before Brody had made a trip down to see her.

"My mom was seventeen when she had me." Ricky volunteered the information after a lull in conversation. "She and my dad never married."

That meant Ricky's mom was a year younger than Brody. "You see much of your dad?"

"No." Ricky rubbed his finger along a scratch in the table. "My mom doesn't like my dad visiting us." A swath of red swept across the kid's cheeks as if he was embarrassed his parents didn't get along. There were always two sides to every breakup—except in Brody's case. He had no one to blame but himself after Kelly had walked out on him.

Skipping the fatherhood inquiries, Brody asked, "Do you help your mother shoe horses?"

"Sometimes. Mostly I muck the barn."

"Does your mom work for herself?"

"You sure are nosy."

"Sorry." He blamed his prying on the fact that he hadn't had a decent conversation with another human being in a week. "Guess I miss having someone to shoot the bull with."

"You could get a dog."

Brody chuckled. "You gotta dog?"

"Yeah. Spot helps calm the horses when my mom's working with them."

"What kind of dog is Spot?"

"Blue heeler. He was my great-grandpa's dog."

Was? "Something happen to your great-grandfather?"

"He died a few years ago."

"Where's your grandfather?"

"I don't know. I've never met him."

The teen's great-grandpa was dead. His father was a deadbeat dad. And his grandfather had never been in the picture. Brody had better stop with the questions before he learned too much. Getting close to people wasn't in anyone's best interest—especially his.

"Let's see if one of the other contestants has bagged a pig." They joined the people gathering near the corral. A cow bell clanged and the crowd quieted.

"We've got two winners today! Brody Murphy and his partner Ricky Sovo. Mike Stern and his partner Bob Benington."

Damn. Brody decided some money was better than none.

He collected the two hundred-fifty dollars and forked over the kid's share. "Been nice doing business with you, Ricky." He tipped his hat, then headed for the parking lot.

Brody drove back through town to gas up and waited

five minutes in line before his turn at the pump. He went inside to pay for fifty dollars worth of gas and a Twinkie. While the fuel pumped, he perused the PRCA schedule for the end of March and beginning of April. He might consider one event if he could scratch together the two-hundred-dollar entry fee.

The pump kicked off and Brody moved the truck to a parking space in front of the convenience store. He ate his Twinkie and people-watched. A pair of past-their-prime biker chicks pulled into the station on Harleys. Decked out from head to toe in leather and chains both women had jet-black hair and more wrinkles than a shar-pei pooch.

A movement out of the corner of Brody's eye caught his attention. A little girl, not more than a few feet tall, stood on her tiptoes next to the trash can outside the store and threw away a fast-food bag. She turned and smiled—in that instant Brody was swept back in time. His lungs tightened painfully as he watched the girl's father scoop her into his arms. His gaze remained glued to the pair as the giggling child hugged her father.

Eyes burning, Brody recalled the last time his daughter had hugged him—Angel had wound her slim arms around his neck the night he'd carried her to the truck to drive her to the emergency room. They'd arrived at the hospital over an hour later, but Angel hadn't had the strength to open her eyes. Two years had passed since his five-year-old daughter's death. When would Brody stop seeing Angel in every blond-haired little girl who crossed his path? How far did he have to run to escape the memories?

The past few months had been pure hell while he

waited for the rodeo season to pick up—too much time between rides and nowhere to go. No one to talk to. No one to distract him from the past.

Quit feeling sorry for yourself. You made choices. You have to live with the consequences.

The moment the girl and her father pulled away, Brody started the truck and left the gas station. He'd driven a mile out of town when he observed his hog-catching partner thumbing rides along the side of the road.

What the heck was Ricky doing hitchhiking? Yeah, Brody had bummed a few rides in his time but this wasn't rural Montana. Bandera was less than forty miles from San Antonio and there was a lot of traffic along the highway, making it dangerous. Heck, anyone who'd downed one too many beers at the festival might easily swerve out of their lane and hit the kid. Brody drove past Ricky and glanced in the rearview mirror. The kid flashed his middle finger. Chuckling, Brody pulled onto the shoulder and lowered the passenger-side window.

Ricky caught up and poked his head inside the truck. "Thanks for the—oh, it's you."

"Want a lift or not?"

Ricky got in and buckled up.

"Home?" Brody asked.

"Yeah."

"Which way?"

"The Wild Rose." The kid pointed out the windshield. "'Bout five miles up the road there's a turnoff."

Five miles. The teen had made quite a hike into Bandera. After checking to see that the coast was clear,

Brody pulled back onto the highway. "Don't you have a bicycle?"

"Nope."

"I guess it won't be long before you earn a driver's license."

"Like that's gonna matter." Ricky snorted. "My mom doesn't make enough money for us to buy a second car."

Letting the subject drop, Brody pumped up the radio volume. The miles flew by then he turned down River Ranch Drive.

"The entrance is up on the left," Ricky said.

Brody whistled low between his teeth as the truck sped past rich, green pastureland. A billboard advertised Organic Hay 4-Sale and a hundred yards later a second sign listed Horses 4-Sale. This was no start-up horse ranch.

The words Wild Rose Ranch were carved into the twenty-foot iron gate that guarded the entrance. A limestone wall ran a half mile in both directions before giving way to traditional pasture fencing. The gate had been left open, so Brody drove through. "What kinds of horses do they raise here?"

"Palominos, buckskins and paints."

The road cut through fenced-in pastures where horses grazed. Live oak, red oak and bur oak trees dotted the landscape, providing shade from the sun. Brody studied the ranch buildings as he pulled into the yard. White-washed paddocks sat between two immense barns—one for the horses and one for equipment. The pristine condition of the structures convinced him that Wild Rose horseflesh went for top dollar.

A woman stepped from the horse barn, a dog by her side. The lady's features were hidden by the shadow the late-afternoon sun cast across the front of the building.

"That's my mom and Spot. Thanks for the ride."

Before Brody had a chance to speak, Ricky jumped out of the truck and hurried toward a small cabin in the distance. The woman called Ricky's name, but the kid ignored her.

Truck idling, Brody debated his next move as two wranglers galloped at full speed into the yard. The men hitched their horses to the water trough then cast puzzled looks Brody's way as they stalked toward Ricky's mother. Spot's ears perked and his tail stopped wagging.

The cowboys' stiff postures and scowling faces put Brody on alert. He lowered the windows then shut off the truck engine and eavesdropped on the group's conversation.

Both men spoke at once—one using wild arm gestures, the other jabbing his finger at Ricky's mother, forcing her to retreat a step. Without considering the consequences, Brody left the truck.

This wasn't his fight he told himself, but his feet kept moving toward the barn. Within a few yards of the trio, he cleared his throat. The bickering ceased and all eyes focused on him.

Brody flashed his pearly whites. "What seems to be the problem?"

Chapter Two

"Who the hell are you?"

Kat cringed at Roger Buckingham's rudeness. The redheaded cowpuncher with a pockmarked face spit tobacco juice at the ground, barley missing the stranger's boot.

"Brody Murphy." He held out his hand.

Brody Murphy... Kat studied the handsome cowboy who'd dropped her son off moments ago. He didn't look familiar. She'd been shoeing horses in the area for years and the name Brody Murphy had never come up in her conversations with the locals. "I'm Katarina Sovo." Brody Murphy's callused fingers squeezed her hand firmly—not gently as if he feared her bones would break. Her respect for the man upped a notch.

He smiled, only this time with their fingers entwined, Kat felt a jolt of electricity race up her arm. She blamed her reaction on the fact that she was in the middle of a long dry spell when it came to male companionship. The last man she'd been involved with had soured her on the gender and she'd decided she was done with the opposite sex—especially the handsome ones. Brody Murphy released her hand, and automatically Kat curled her fingers into a fist to retain the warmth from his touch.

"I was passing through town when I met Ricky at the festival in Mansfield Park."

Kat hadn't even realized Ricky had left the ranch until Brody had driven into the yard with her son in the front seat of his truck. Ricky couldn't have picked a worst time to pull a disappearing stunt. "Thank you for bringing him home."

"No problem."

"We done chitchattin'?" Roger glared.

"It appears you three are having a disagreement," Brody said. "Maybe I can help settle the dispute."

"Butt out, mister. This ain't none of your business." Clyde Nyman, Roger's balding, bowlegged sidekick, sneered.

Kat rocked onto the balls of her feet in an attempt to appear taller—not an easy task when she barely topped five-three. "The Bakers left me in charge and—"

"That don't mean you get to call all the shots." Clyde added his tobacco spit to the puddle forming in front of Brody Murphy's boot, then leaned forward, crowding Kat.

Spot growled. "It's okay, boy." Kat scratched the dog's graying head. Arthritis had slowed the twelve-year-old heeler, but his protective instincts were as keen as ever. Spot wouldn't hesitate to attack Roger or Clyde if they threatened her or Ricky.

"Where I come from—" Brody joined Kat's side, providing a united front against the ranch hands "—the person in charge does call the shots."

"Mister, nobody cares where you come from," Clyde said.

"Montana."

The handsome drifter was a long way from home.

"We do things different-like down here in Texas." Roger swung his gaze to Kat. "The Bakers hired us to work with their horses not plow fields."

The Wild Rose Ranch was well-known for their superb horseflesh and organic hay. Horse owners from all over the state purchased the expensive feed for their prized livestock. Before the Bakers had departed on their European vacation, they'd put Kat in charge. Had she known the two hands would object to taking direction from a woman, she might have refused the temporary promotion.

No, you wouldn't have. Kat rubbed her brow and prayed for patience. She had a lot riding on her ability to keep the ranch running smoothly while the owners were away. Only a week into the job and already she had a crisis on her hands. "They're predicting rain—"

"The weather isn't our problem." Roger removed his hat and smacked it against his thigh, sending dust particles dancing in the air around him.

"That's right," Clyde said. "We're not raking hay for no stinkin' female."

"Watch your mouth, fella. That's no way to speak to a lady."

"Like my pardner said, this ain't none of your beeswax." Roger glared.

"You threaten Ms. Sovo and I'll make it my beeswax."

Kat wasn't used to having a man stand up for her, and Brody coming to her defense left her speechless.

"What're you gonna do? Horsewhip us?" Clyde taunted.

"Enough bickering." Although Brody meant well, Kat refused to allow him to take control of a situation he knew nothing about. "If you won't bring in the hay, then there's no reason to remain on the Wild Rose payroll." She gripped Spot's collar and prayed the threat of unemployment would end the cowboys' mutiny.

Roger stepped forward, but Brody blocked his path. "You were given a choice. Drive a tractor or walk off the job." Brody might be shorter than Roger, but the cowboy was made of solid muscle. Roger would be wise to think twice about picking a fight with the stranger.

"You're gonna regret this." Roger stomped off, Clyde dogging his heels. The men collected their saddles and gear then tossed them into the bed of a late-model Ford. The truck sped off, spewing bits of gravel across the driveway.

Oh, Lord. She'd lost her mind. No capable foreman would permit her employees to walk off the job and leave a ranch shorthanded. Aside from a horse with an abscess that needed daily attention, Kat now had fifty acres of hay waiting to be mowed.

"You're not going to cry because those guys quit, are you?"

Men. They were clueless dopes when it came to understanding women. Anger, not self-pity caused Kat's eyes to water. Irritated with Brody Murphy for sticking his nose where it didn't belong she spun on her boot heel and retreated to the foreman's cabin.

"Wait up."

Kat stopped and Brody plowed into her back.

"Sorry," he muttered.

Hands on her hips, she faced the cowboy. "Roger and Clyde might be idiots, but thanks to you I'm undermanned."

"I didn't fire them. You did."

"Only because you opened your big mouth."

"Those guys are losers. The ranch owners will be relieved to be rid of them."

Not likely. Kat doubted the Bakers would be thrilled when they learned she'd run off their employees and the organic hay sat rotting in the field. *Shoot*. The Bakers had offered Kat an opportunity to prove she deserved a permanent position at the Wild Rose. Putting her in charge of the ranch while they jet-setted through Europe was a test—one she couldn't afford to fail.

She needed the security of a salaried job. As Wild Rose's farrier she'd no longer be forced to drag her son on the road with her as she traveled from ranch to ranch shoeing horses. Instead of being homeschooled Ricky would have an opportunity to attend the junior high in Bandera and make lasting friendships.

There was another perk that came with the job—the foreman's cabin. She and Ricky wouldn't have to live in the old trailer they'd called home since her grandfather's death. There were plenty of benefits to putting down roots at the Wild Rose, but Roger and Clyde quitting threatened all her hopes and dreams.

"Ricky!" she hollered toward the open window at the front of the cabin. No answer. She yelled louder. "Get your backside out here right now, young man!"

Almost a minute passed before the front door opened. Her sullen son shuffled down the porch steps. "I need your…" Her eyes rounded. "Why is your lip swollen?"

Ricky pointed to Brody, reminding Kat that the cowboy hadn't left. "You hit my son?"

"No!" Brody scowled at Ricky. "He bumped into me during the hog-catching contest."

"Hog contest?" Kat swung her gaze between the two males.

"She's gonna get mad at me," Ricky warned Brody.

"Bandera's Wild Hog Explosion," Brody said.

"I can't believe you walked all the way into Bandera." Kat glared at her son.

"Some dude on a Harley gave me a ride into town and Brody brought me back." Ricky shrugged. "No big deal."

Clenching her teeth, Kat counted to ten. She ought to tan the rascal's hide for hitchhiking, but she didn't have the heart because she suspected Ricky had sneaked off hoping to find his father. Dwayne had promised to take him to the festival this past Valentine's Day when he'd stopped by the trailer for an unannounced visit. Kat wished Ricky would wake up and realize his father couldn't be counted on for anything.

"I would have driven you into town. All you had to do was ask, young man."

"No, you wouldn't. You're always too busy."

At moments like this, Kat really missed her grandfather. Ricky had respected and obeyed his great-grandfather in all things. "Next time you decide to leave the ranch, you check with me first."

"Your mother's right. Thumbing rides is dangerous and so is talking to strangers."

Ricky gaped at Brody. "You talked to me first."

"You're lucky I meant you no harm." Brody raised an eyebrow. "Not everyone is as cordial as me."

When Brody turned his smile in Kat's direction, she swore the day's mild temperature spiked ten degrees. "I don't have time to stand here and argue. We'll talk about this during supper, Ricky. Right now I need you to clean the stalls."

"Why?"

"Two of the hands quit. Instead of working with the horses tomorrow I'll be mowing hay."

"This sucks."

It sure does.

"Why don't you hire him?" Ricky nodded to Brody.

"Hold up, kid. I'm not looking for work." Brody stared at his watch. "As a matter of fact I'm on my way to Lubbock."

"What for?" Ricky asked.

"A rodeo."

"Brody's a bull rider," Ricky explained to Kat.

She'd been correct in assuming Brody was a drifter. Rodeo cowboys—the serious contenders—traveled the circuit most of the year. Kat clasped her son's shoulder. "The wheelbarrow is parked by the compost pile." She waited until he rounded the corner of the barn, then spoke. "Thank you for looking out for my son today and good luck in Lubbock."

Brody caught Kat's arm before she'd taken a step. "I guess I could help—"

"Don't." She yanked her arm free.

"Don't what?"

Kat was used to men equating her small stature with weakness. "Don't assume I'm some helpless woman who needs a knight in shining armor to rescue her."

"That wasn't—"

"I've been on my own a long time and I don't need a man's help."

"Yes, ma'am." Brody tipped his hat. "I'll leave you to your business." He returned to his truck and drove away.

Brody backing off so easily reaffirmed Kat's belief that handsome cowboys were a waste of time. She ought to know—Ricky's father had used his good looks and charm to take her for a ride, then had tucked tail and run after she'd turned up pregnant.

Cowboys. Who needed them?

BRODY COULDN'T GET away from the Wild Rose fast enough. He turned right onto River Ranch Road and hit the accelerator. What had gotten into him—offering to help Ricky muck the barn?

The road came to a T and Brody stopped. He stared through the windshield at the limestone rock formation across the highway. What a weird day this had been. He'd begun with the best of intentions—accepting Drew's offer to work at Dry Creek Acres. Instead, he'd found himself in Bandera teaming up with a teenager in a hog-catching contest. Then to top it off he'd stuck his nose in Katarina Sovo's business.

Katarina—sounded like a ballerina's name.

His mind conjured up an image of Ricky's mother.

Once he'd gotten an eyeful of the woman he'd almost swallowed his tongue—a rare event for a man used to beautiful women chasing after him. He appreciated Katarina's midnight-black ponytail, tanned skin, slanted brown eyes and high cheekbones, but it had been her fighting spirit that had bowled him over.

Katarina Sovo was no wilting flower. Her short, sturdy frame had flaunted a toned physique. The hint of bicep muscle beneath her T-shirt proved she made her living outdoors and not behind a desk. He could easily picture her hoisting a sixty-pound saddle onto the back of a horse without losing her breath.

That Ricky's mother hadn't succumbed to Brody's charms had amused him. She was the first woman since his ex who'd been immune to his handsome face. Deciding he'd wasted enough time contemplating the woman, Brody drove west away from Bandera. He blasted the radio, hoping the noise would muffle any lingering thoughts of the feisty foreman.

He'd driven ten miles when signs advertising Dicky's Roadhouse sprouted up every hundred yards along the road. Why not? Now that he had a little jingle in his pocket, he'd sit a spell, drink a beer and plan out his rodeo schedule for the upcoming month. A few minutes later he parked in the dirt lot in front of a machine-shed building that had been converted into a bar.

Inside, music blared from the jukebox and cigarette smoke clouded the air—apparently no-smoking laws didn't apply to this Texas dive. Brody sidled up to the bar, ordered a longneck then made his way through the crowd to the outdoor patio in back. All of the tables were taken, so he stood in the corner partially concealed by a low-hanging awning.

Bits and pieces of conversation drifted in one ear and out the other—talk about jobs, baseball and the Bandera festival. Halfway through his beer Brody made up his mind to catch the rodeo in Abilene next Friday. He could use a warm-up ride before competing in Lubbock that Saturday. A stray cat picking through the garbage that overflowed the waste barrel at the back of the lot caught his attention. The skinny gray-and-white fur ball batted about an empty sardine can, then scurried away when a larger tabby wandered out from beneath a nearby bush.

"That bitch is gonna regret sendin' us packin'."

The hairs on the back of Brody's neck stood on end. He recognized the voices of the cowboys Katarina had fired. The men shared a pitcher of beer at a table close by. Keeping to the shadows, Brody tuned his ear to their conversation.

"Shit, I'm no damned farmer." Clyde voiced the complaint.

"I shoulda been put in charge," Roger grumbled. "Don't my hard work these past five years count for somethin'?"

Clyde chugged his beer, then reached for the pitcher. "Word's gonna spread we walked off the job and won't no one hire us."

"Don't worry. After that bitch makes a mess of things, we'll show up 'n' save the day." Roger chuckled. "Mark my words she'll beg us to come back and when she does, we'll demand a pay raise."

"What if she don't make a mess of things?" Clyde's whiny voice grated on Brody's nerves.

"We're gonna see to it she does." Roger flashed a menacing smirk before signaling the waitress for a second pitcher of beer. Their conversation shifted to Clyde's brother Earl who'd recently been released from prison and was having a tough time finding employment. Brody quit listening.

Now what?

They're not your problem. Let someone else rescue them.

He didn't dare leave the area, knowing that Katarina might be a sitting duck for the duo's pranks. Brody had no choice but to return to the Wild Rose and warn Ricky's mother about the cowboys' threat.

OUT OF THE CORNER of her eye, Kat watched Ricky pitch clean hay into the horse stall at the far end of the barn. She hated that her relationship with her teenage son had become strained these past few months. Was it only yesterday that Ricky had shadowed her and his great-grandfather chattering their ears off? Since Ricky had hit puberty she'd felt useless as a parent. Her son needed another man in his life to talk to about guy stuff—girls, sex, cars. Too bad Ricky couldn't count on his father to be there for him.

Dwayne did more harm than good when he spent time with their son. His hit-or-miss visits did nothing more than show Ricky he wasn't a priority in his father's life. If Kat expected a permanent position at the Wild Rose she had to demonstrate to the Bakers that she had her life under control. Ricky's jaunt into town today proved the opposite.

If Kat believed her son would settle down soon, she was dreaming. When her back was turned he'd take off again in search of his father, only the next time he might not be lucky enough to run into a stranger as trustworthy as Brody Murphy. Brody... She shook her head to dispel the handsome cowboy's face from her memory.

She returned her attention to Tiger's hoof, which soaked in a bucket of warm water and antiseptic. "Let me see, Tiger." Kat lifted the gelding's hoof and examined the swelling. "Better." She set the hoof in the water and scratched Tiger behind the ears. "Ten more minutes."

After rescuing the horse from an abusive owner, the Bakers discovered that Tiger had been improperly shod. The neglect had resulted in a nasty abscess, which prevented the gelding from putting weight on his leg. Scott Clark, the area's large-animal veterinarian had treated Tiger with antibiotics then Kat had been put in charge of restoring the hoof to good health. She'd applied all the usual remedies, which cleared up the infection, but when she placed a new shoe on the hoof, the swelling returned.

Kat wished her grandfather was still alive. She'd learned all about shoeing horses and then some from him. He'd know why Tiger's abscess wouldn't heal. She yearned to prove to the Bakers that their horses were in capable hands, but if the gelding's hoof didn't heal soon, Kat would be forced to concede defeat and seek the vet's advice. Luckily she and Scott Clark were good friends.

By the time Kat had turned eighteen, Ricky had already celebrated his first birthday. Although her grandparents had helped Kat care for the baby, she hadn't handled motherhood well the first few years. When Scott had offered her a job as his assistant, she'd jumped at the chance to tag along on his ranch calls and escape the constant demands of caring for a small child.

Thinking back on that time in her life, Kat acknowledged that she'd resented being burdened with raising Ricky while Dwayne had come and gone—mostly gone—as he'd pleased. She, not Dwayne, had changed diapers, washed baby clothes and paced the floor for hours at a time when Ricky had suffered one of his frequent bouts of colic.

Shortly after Ricky turned four Kat's grandmother had died, forcing Kat to take full responsibility for her son 24/7. The first few months had been pure hell—not for her but poor Ricky. Her son had cried nonstop for his *abuela* and refused to be consoled by Kat. Kat had turned to her grandfather for help but he'd been too consumed with grief, forcing her and Ricky to find their way as mother and son all on their own.

Kat had been tempted to follow in her mother's footsteps and run from her responsibility to her child, but each time Kat had packed her bag Ricky's sad blue eyes had changed her mind. Then almost a year to the day her grandmother had died, Ricky had hugged Kat and said, "I love you, Mama." From that moment on Ricky became the center of Kat's world—her purpose for living. Her every act and decision was made with his best interests in mind. As with most mothers and sons, she and Ricky had experienced their share of ups and downs through the years, but each night she thanked God for blessing her life with him.

"What's for supper?" Ricky's question startled Kat.

She threw out a peace offering. "I can make Grandpa's Mexican casserole." The dish was Ricky's favorite—rice, refried beans, taco meat, black olives and a can of hot enchilada sauce mixed together and baked with a thick layer of cheddar cheese on top.

"Okay." Ricky pushed the wheelbarrow out of the barn and Kat followed, Spot bringing up the rear.

"You can't leave the ranch and not tell me where you're going," she said while he emptied the barrow.

"Jeez, Mom. Nothing happened."

"That's beside the point. I have to know where you are at all times. What if there's an emergency at the ranch and I need your help?"

"Ask one of the other hands."

Hand not hands. Roger's and Clyde's departure had left Kat with one cowboy—Melissa Baker's younger brother, Wes. Wes had a drinking problem—the main reason the Bakers had put Kat in charge of the ranch. Checking the fence line for breaks and making sure the water tanks were full in the pastures was about all Wes could handle.

"Whether help is nearby or not doesn't matter, Ricky. I—"

"He wasn't there, Mom." Her son's voice broke. "Dad said we'd team up for the hog-catching contest, but he never showed."

Kat ached for Ricky. Damn Dwayne Walker and his lazy ass.

"You told him to stay away from me." Ricky's accusing eyes pinned her. "That's why he didn't come."

"I said to keep away from the Wild Rose, not from you." Dwayne's visits were taking a toll on Ricky. Birthdays and holidays came and went without presents, calls or visits. If Dwayne happened to drop in on her and Ricky, he spent the time sitting in the trailer watching TV. Once he'd eaten all of Kat's food he took off. Kat had never known her own father and she'd been certain Dwayne showing up once in a blue moon was better than not being in the picture at all. Ricky's forlorn expression proved her good intentions had failed miserably. She should have kicked Dwayne out of their lives years ago, and saved her and Ricky a lot of heartache and money.

"If the Bakers give you a permanent job here, can Dad visit me as much as he wants?"

"Within reason." They'd been at the Wild Rose since January and Kat was working hard to prove she deserved long-term work at the ranch. But she was doing it for her and Ricky—not to give Dwayne a place to crash when he was between girlfriends. Kat wanted Ricky to be able to attend school in Bandera this fall, hoping that if he became involved in sports and clubs he'd be too busy to care how often his father visited. The Wild Rose was the answer to all their problems, but Kat needed Ricky's cooperation to succeed. "Promise me you won't run off again."

Instead of reassuring Kat, Ricky stared over her shoulder.

Kat spun and shielded her eyes against the late-afternoon sun.

The bull rider was back.

Chapter Three

Kat worried her lower lip as Ricky raced toward Brody Murphy's red Dodge. The cowboy was practically a stranger but she feared her son had targeted the bull rider as his new idol.

The instant the driver-side door opened, Ricky hollered, "Why'd you come back, Brody?"

"Hey, kid." Brody and her son exchanged fist pumps then his gaze—shielded by aviator sunglasses—met Kat's across the hood of the pickup. He flashed his Hollywood smile and her pulse quickened. As Brody closed the gap between them, she reminded herself that the last thing she needed right now was the distraction of a handsome man.

"Forget something?" she asked when he stopped in front of her.

He removed his glasses and serious brown eyes studied her. "We need to talk." The sober note in his voice concerned Kat.

"Hey, Brody." Ricky tugged the cowboy's shirtsleeve. "My mom's gonna make my great-grandpa's Mexican casserole for supper. You wanna eat with us?"

Oh, Ricky, why did you—

"Thanks, but I can't stay. I came back to tell your mom something."

"What?" Ricky's gaze bounced between the adults.

"Never mind, young man. Go finish your chores," Kat said.

"I already mucked the stalls."

"Then top off the feed bins and change out the water buckets." "C'mon, Spot." Muttering beneath his breath, Ricky stomped off.

Motioning for Brody to follow, Kat walked up to the foreman's cabin. At the porch steps she said, "I have iced tea or soda."

"Don't bother. I'm fine."

The cowboy wasn't much for socializing. Kat sat in the rocker nearest the door. Brody leaned against the railing across from her—his crotch eye level with Kat's gaze. It took more willpower than she'd expected to ignore the way the faded denim jeans molded to his thighs.

"I thought you were on your way to Lubbock," she said.

"I was. Am." He removed his hat and ran his fingers through his sandy-blond hair. He needed a trim, but the shaggy style fit his movie star looks. "I stopped at Dicky's Roadhouse outside of Bandera and bumped into the two cowboys who walked off the job."

"Roger and Clyde didn't walk off, I fired them." *Because your interference forced my hand.*

Brody shrugged as if he didn't care one way or the other how the ranch hands had been relieved of their positions. "I listened in on their chat and they intend to make trouble for you."

"What kind of trouble?" Kat straightened in her seat.

"They didn't mention specifics, but they want you to fail, so you'll be forced to hire them back. And when you do, they'll demand a pay raise."

Damn their lazy hides. She didn't have time to run helter-skelter around the ranch, keeping an eye out for Clyde's and Roger's shenanigans. She had enough on her plate caring for the horses and harvesting the hay. "Are you sure you heard right?"

"Positive. That's why I returned, so you could register a complaint with the sheriff's department."

"Thanks for the warning but I won't be notifying Sheriff Conrad." The sixty-five-year-old man was a throwback to the Chisholm Trail days.

"Mind if I ask why?"

Yes. "The sheriff can't do anything if Clyde and Roger haven't committed a crime." If she spoke to the sheriff now, the lawman would assume she was paranoid or worse—a ditzy female.

"I disagree."

She sprang from the chair and paced to the end of the porch. "In case it's slipped your notice I'm a woman working in a man's—"

"No."

Kat blinked. "No what?"

"No, it did not escape my notice that you're a woman." An appreciative once-over accompanied his statement.

Ignoring the heat suffusing her face, Kat continued. "If I report what you overheard, Sheriff Conrad will notify the Bakers and they'll cut their vacation short."

And end Kat's chance of making the Wild Rose her and Ricky's permanent home.

"Katarina, if those two doofuses decide to make good on their threat…"

The husky way her name slid off Brody's tongue messed with Kat's concentration. "I'm sorry, say that again."

"Guys like Roger and Clyde are dangerous. They're stupid enough to hurt someone. They might only want to scare you, but a practical joke can easily get out of hand."

Brody was right. She couldn't stand back and wait for trouble, but informing the authorities was out of the question—for now. She'd have to find a way to outsmart the pesky ranch hands. "I'll warn Wes to keep an eye out for any unusual activity."

"Who's Wes?"

"Melissa Baker's younger brother. He lives in the line shack at the south end of the ranch."

"He's not going to be much help if Clyde and Roger decided to mess with the barns."

"They wouldn't dare harm the horses."

"Are you willing to chance it? What if they contaminate the feed or—"

"Stop." She held up her hand.

"I'm sorry, Kata—"

"It's Kat." Brody's use of her full name sounded too intimate.

"Take my advice and get help…Kat."

Kat was a fighter and refused to cower in the face of empty threats. On the other hand, it wouldn't hurt, to have an extra pair of eyes watching over the ranch until the Bakers returned. Brown eyes the color of dark chocolate stared Kat down. A solution with a million drawbacks formed in her mind. *No... Not Brody.* Any man but the sexy one in front of her. "You could stay."

He flinched as if she'd peppered his hide with buckshot.

The more Kat pondered the idea, the more it made sense. "You and Ricky can harvest the hay, while I work with the horses and keep an eye on the barn."

"You don't know anything about me," Brody said.

I know you were kind to my son. You worry about others—or else you wouldn't have driven back to the Wild Rose to warn me about Clyde and Roger. And you're easy on the eyes—not that Brody's good looks had anything to do with her offer. Kat wasn't in the market for a man and her responsibilities at the ranch allowed little time for a personal life.

"I could be a serial killer. A rapist. An ex-con."

"Are you any of those things?" she asked.

"Hell, no."

Her woman's intuition never failed her. She'd known Dwayne was a wild one when they'd dated in high school, but she'd taken a chance on him anyway. After she'd broken the news that he'd gotten her pregnant, she'd hoped he'd settle down and help her raise Ricky, but her instincts had proven correct again—Dwayne had walked away from his responsibilities. She sensed Brody was a better man than Ricky's father—an upstanding guy and a hard worker.

"I trust you not to harm me or my son." The silence that followed Kat's statement tied her stomach in knots. "I can offer you room and board and a decent wage."

With two cowboys off the payroll, she could afford to give Brody a little more than the average allowance for ranch hands.

"A job would interfere with my rodeo schedule."

"You could work here during the week and rodeo on the weekends." The rodeo cowboys she'd run into over the years usually hired on as ranch hands to earn entry-fee money.

"I'm sorry." He shoved away from the rail and skirted past her. "I can't stay."

Before his boot landed on the first step, Kat asked, "Is it Lubbock? Do you have a girlfriend or a wife and family there?" Brody didn't wear a wedding ring—then again a lot of cowboys never bothered with them.

"The only thing waiting for me in Lubbock is a rodeo."

Why the news pleased Kat, she couldn't say.

Brody descended a second step.

"The trailer comes with a hot shower." She pointed to the vintage 1965 Silver Streak that had belonged to her grandfather. Kat had seen the dirty laundry, fast-food wrappers and the sleeping bag piled in the backseat of his truck and guessed the Dodge Ram had been Brody's home for a while. Shoot, he probably hadn't slept in a real bed in months.

His boot clomped against the third step.

Okay, so the Silver Streak wasn't five-star accommodations, but the bed linens were fresh and he was welcome to use the washer and dryer in the cabin to do his laundry. "If you stay, Ricky won't run off again when I turn my back." Kat felt awful for laying that at Brody's feet, but the older Ricky got the more he wanted to be with his father. Today's jaunt into Bandera had been a warning sign that one day soon her son would strike out on his own to find Dwayne. She hated using Brody, but if his hanging around distracted Ricky maybe he'd forget about searching for his father—at least for a little while.

Brody's boot hit the ground.

"Stay for supper." Kat quickly moved down the steps and squared off with him. "I owe you a dinner for watching out for Ricky today and warning us about Clyde and Roger."

As if he'd been holding his breath for minutes not seconds, the air exploded from Brody's chest. "I guess I could eat something."

Now that Kat had stalled his departure, her other senses kicked in and she caught the crisp scent of Brody's aftershave—an unusual smell for a hardworking cowboy. "I'll ring the bell when supper's ready."

Kat watched Brody retreat to the barn. She'd won the first round. If *she* couldn't change Brody's mind about staying, then hopefully Grandpa's Mexican casserole would.

BRODY STOOD IN THE shadows inside the barn, waiting for his eyes to adjust to the dim interior. He watched Ricky scoop feed from a large bin near a storage room. Instead of announcing his presence, Brody took a moment to gather his wits—he'd need them if he intended to leave the ranch and not look back following supper.

Today had felt like the longest day of his life and it wasn't finished yet. Instead of poking his nose where it didn't belong, he should have minded his own business after he'd delivered Ricky to the Wild Rose.

Kat... The woman intrigued Brody, but he was nuts to consider working for her even on a temporary basis. Earning a regular paycheck would come in handy for covering his rodeo fees and home-cooked meals and hot showers sounded mighty good. But gut instinct insisted that a few creature comforts weren't worth the risk of getting to know Kat and Ricky on a personal level.

The one place Brody truly felt comfortable was on the road. Traveling the circuit prevented him from investing in relationships. Drew had been the only person Brody had gotten close to since Angel's death and his subsequent divorce from Kelly. The invite to Dry Creek Acres had been Drew's attempt to make Brody an extended family member. What if Kat's invitation ended up the same as Drew's? Brody had quit being part of a family after Angel had died. The last thing he wanted to do was live and work where every day he'd be reminded of what he'd lost and would never again have.

"You gonna stand there or help?"

Ricky's voice interrupted Brody's thoughts. "I don't know, kid. I kinda like watching you work."

"Ha, ha."

"What do you want me to do?" Brody moved farther into the barn.

"The horses need fresh water."

"I'm on it." The barn floor consisted of a cement slab with a two-inch grated drain running through the middle. All Brody had to do was tip the buckets onto their sides and the dirty water ran down the drain. The horse stalls were equipped with automated feeders that dispensed set amounts of feed at scheduled intervals throughout the day. Not even the Black Stone Ranch in Montana, which ran ten thousand head of Aberdeen Angus, boasted a modern barn such as this one.

"Hose is up there." Ricky nodded to the post in the center of the barn, where a rubber hose connected to the water pipes overhead.

"You gonna eat with us?" Ricky asked.

"Looks that way."

The teen finished adding grain to the bins then stretched out on a hay bale and watched Brody. "What's it like riding bulls?"

"It mostly hurts."

"Then how come you do it?"

"It's fun if you win." Brody grinned.

"You win a lot?"

"Hardly ever, kid."

"Don't you get scared?"

"Sometimes," Brody admitted. Scared of what might happen if he stopped riding bulls. At thirty-one his rodeo days were numbered.

"You ever get tired of traveling all the time?" Ricky asked.

"Not really." Brody added water to the final bucket then joined the teen on the hay bale. Spot stretched out at their feet and Brody ruffled the dog's wiry gray fur. "I meet a lot of fascinating people. See unique places."

"I hate new places."

"You move a lot?" Brody asked.

"After my great-grandpa died, my mom had to sell his house and we got stuck living in his old trailer." Ricky shoved a piece of straw in his mouth. "I know my mom works hard but I miss not having our own house."

"Does your father help you and your mom?" Brody regretted the question as soon as it slipped out. The less he learned about Kat and Ricky's situation the better for all concerned.

"My dad doesn't have much money." Ricky picked at a clump of dried mud on his jeans. "Mom's lucky 'cause she can make money shoeing horses."

Lucky? People made their own luck by working hard, not by waiting for luck to find them. Ricky's father sounded like a real winner.

Who are you to criticize? Brody's position at the Black Stone Ranch had brought home a steady paycheck for years, but when the opportunity arose to move into Kalispell and hire on with the local meat-processing plant, he'd snubbed his nose at the job. He'd loved working with cattle and had preferred to punch live cows not dead ones. In the end, his wife and daughter had paid a high price because he hadn't wanted to give up being a cowboy.

Brody and Kelly had argued often about the fact that his job as a ranch hand hadn't come with health insurance. Then Angel had fallen ill and he'd insisted Kelly wait until payday to take their daughter to the doctor. They hadn't had the cash to cover the visit and their credit card had been maxed out. By the time Kelly got it through Brody's thick skull that their daughter wasn't getting better, it had been too late.

Forcing his mind from the past, Brody changed the subject. "You play on any sports teams at school?"

"I'm homeschooled."

Brody didn't know much about homeschooling kids. He'd attended public schools until he'd graduated. "What about the Bakers? Do they have kids your age?"

"Nope."

"What do you do with your free time?"

"Sometimes I fish."

"Sounds like you could use a few more hobbies to keep you from becoming bored and running off like you did today."

"I didn't run off." Ricky averted his gaze. "I was going to see my dad."

As he was no expert in the parent department, Brody gave Ricky's father the benefit of the doubt. "Maybe he had car trouble."

"He doesn't have a car. Or a truck."

Jeez, the kid's dad really was on the down-'n'-out. With the possibility of Roger and Clyde stirring up trouble it was important that Ricky keep his mother informed of his whereabouts at all times.

"Your dad might have had to work."

"My dad doesn't have a job."

Rodeo wasn't a steady source of income and all Brody had to his name were the clothes on his back, his truck and his rodeo gear. He couldn't ride bulls forever, but he couldn't see himself holding down a steady job that kept him in one place, either. Brody was ashamed to admit he and Ricky's father were more alike than different.

"How often do you see your father?" Brody didn't know what possessed him to grill the kid with questions—probably too many days and nights conversing with himself as he drove to his next rodeo.

"Every few months I guess."

Hardly seemed fair that Kat had her hands full raising a son, making a living and dealing with Ricky's dad.

"I'm sorry your father didn't show up today, but that's no reason to leave the ranch without telling your mom."

"Yeah, whatever."

Enough said on the subject. "What else can we do to help your mom since she's cooking supper?"

"Clean the buckets she uses to soak the horses' hooves."

"Lead the way." Brody followed Ricky into a room with a large stainless steel sink and shelves stocked with medicines and first-aid supplies for horses. He and Ricky slipped on rubber gloves and washed the dirty buckets stacked in the sink.

"Brody?"

"What?"

"Do you got any kids?"

Brody froze for several seconds, before he found the strength to take a deep breath. "No."

"How come? Don't you like kids?"

He'd loved Angel. Still loved Angel. Would always love Angel. "I like kids just fine, but rodeo and families don't mix."

"Oh."

The teen's one-word response landed like a punch to Brody's gut. Worrying about Ricky's feelings was yet another reason he wouldn't allow Kat to talk him into sticking around the Wild Rose.

"Got plans for that money you won at the festival today?" Brody asked.

"I might buy a new fishing pole."

Brody had never learned to fish because farming had taken all his father's time and energy. As a matter of fact Brody couldn't recall his father teaching him much of anything through the years. If his father had any spare time during the week he spent the hours cleaning farming equipment or making small repairs around the two-bedroom shack that substituted for a home.

The sound of a clanging bell echoed outside the barn. "Supper's ready." Ricky peeled the rubber gloves off and tossed them into the sink. "Race you." He sprinted from the room.

Brody caught himself in the nick of time before he chased after the kid. When he reached the cabin, Ricky waited on the porch barely out of breath. "Got a place for me to wash up?"

"Inside." Ricky held open the door. "Bathroom's down the hall."

"Hurry," Kat said from the kitchen. "Corn bread will be done in less than a minute."

Brody located the bathroom, which contained a single shower stall, small sink and a toilet. Kat had decorated the tiny space with framed photos of her, Ricky and an older couple he assumed were Ricky's great-grandparents. The sight of the pink nightgown hanging on the back of the door gave Brody pause. He hadn't pegged Kat as a *pink* kind of gal—red or black maybe. He returned to the main room to find Ricky seated at the table.

"Anything I can do to help?" Brody asked.

Kat paused in the task of slicing the corn bread. "No thanks." A moment later she set the food on the table. "Iced tea, water or milk?"

"Water's good."

Drinks taken care of, Kat fetched the sour cream and salsa. Brody was aware of Ricky watching him. "Ladies first." He held out Kat's chair.

"Thank you. Ricky pay attention to Mr. Murphy. You might pick up a few pointers on manners."

Ricky rolled his eyes. "Hurry up, Mom. I'm hungry."

Kat and Ricky filled their plates then Brody helped himself. First bite he groaned. Second bite he closed his eyes. Third bite he grinned. "Wow, this is really good."

"Told ya, you'd like it," Ricky said.

Supper passed with little conversation, then Brody and Ricky cleared the table, while Kat stowed the leftovers in the fridge. "Ricky, would you give the horses their carrots tonight?"

"Sure." The kid grabbed the bag of carrots off the counter and left the cabin.

"Coffee?" Kat asked.

"Only if you're having a cup."

While the coffee brewed, Brody wandered about the room, studying the cabin's construction.

"It's nice, isn't it?" Kat delivered two mugs to the table.

"You don't see many homes made log-cabin style anymore. The quality's top-notch." He sipped the hot brew. "What happened to the Wild Rose foreman?"

"He retired." A short pause followed before Kat got down to business. "Have you given thought to my proposal?"

"I don't—"

"Before you say no, I need you to understand how important this opportunity is to me and Ricky." She swept her hand in front of her. "This cabin will be the first real home Ricky and I have had since my grandfather passed away. Living at the Wild Rose means we'll be in one place long enough to put down roots."

As Brody listened to Kat's impassioned speech, warning lights flashed inside his brain.

"If I can prove to the Bakers that I'm capable of running the Wild Rose, then they'll offer me a permanent position here." She rushed on before he could interrupt. "Ricky's been dragged through Central Texas for the past three years. I want him to have a sense of security and not wake up each morning wondering where we're headed next." Kat locked gazes with Brody. "I can't do that without your help. Please stay until the Bakers come home the middle of May."

May was two months away! "I'm not good at staying in one place long."

"Then hang around until you get the itch to leave."

If Kat found out about his past, he'd be the last person on earth she'd ask for help. Brody knew from his earlier conversation in the barn with Ricky that Kat couldn't count on the boy's father. Her grandfather was dead. Brody had no idea what had happened to her parents, but they weren't in the picture.

It's been a long time since you've thought of anyone but yourself.

"I don't expect you to change your rodeo schedule," Kat said.

Lubbock was a heck of a long way from Bandera, but

there was a smaller rodeo close by in San Marcos two weeks from today. He could catch that one.

"Work here for a few days." Kat fought a smile. "If you don't like taking orders from me, then you can leave. No hard feelings."

Eight weeks wasn't forever, and like Kat said, he could go anytime...no ill will. "Okay. I'll stay." A shiver racked Brody's body. Was his desire to help Kat a signal he was tired of running?

He didn't dare stop running—unless he was ready to face the past.

He wasn't.

Chapter Four

"Well, howdy-doody, Ms. Katarina." Tom Wheeler, the owner of Wheeler Feed & Tack in Bandera greeted Kat Sunday morning.

Tom was an annoying pervert, who insisted on calling Kat by her proper first name when she'd specifically requested he use the shortened version.

"Morning, Mr. Wheeler." Kat didn't have time for small talk. She was in a rush to check on Brody's progress in the hay field back at the Wild Rose.

"How've you and your boy been?" Tom's shadow fell over Kat as she searched the shelves for the supplies on her list.

"Fine." She edged sideways, putting an extra foot of space between her and the owner. On the few occasions she'd visited the store, Tom had faked a stumble and bumped into a part of her body he had no business coming in contact with. She'd considered mentioning his inappropriate behavior to Melissa Baker but Tom was the kind of man who'd turn the tables on Kat and insist she'd given off signals that welcomed his advances. No sense stirring up trouble when Wheeler Tack & Feed was the nearest supply store to the ranch.

"Roger and Clyde stopped by the other day and said they'd quit the Wild Rose."

So the deserters were still in the area. "They didn't quit. I fired them because they refused to take orders from me."

"That's not how they see it."

Of course not. Men were delusional. She grabbed a large bag of Epsom salts and a bottle of Betadine solution then shoved them into Tom's arms before moving down the aisle to inspect the first aid supplies.

"Those two are angrier than a Texas diamondback with a squished rattle."

"They can have their jobs back at any time as long as they agree to follow orders." Kat added a box of gauze to her purchases.

"Now, Katarina—" Tom shook his head and stared at Kat as if she were simple in the head "—you know real cowboys don't take orders from women."

"Is that so?" Kat propped her fists on her hips and squared off with Tom. "I've got a real cowboy out at the Wild Rose right now working for me and he took my orders this morning without complaint."

As a matter of fact, Brody had surprised Kat when he'd shown up for breakfast at sunrise. He'd offered to make the coffee while she'd whipped up a batch of pancakes. Kat couldn't remember the last time she'd had a man's help fixing breakfast.

"Where'd you find this cowboy?"

"He was passing through the area."

"You gotta be careful these days, Katarina." A tsk-tsking sound echoed in the air. "There's all kind of crazy folk out there ready to take advantage of a woman like you."

Kat found the duct tape and resisted the urge to slap a piece across Tom's mouth. "What do you mean a woman like me?"

"You know…a woman all alone with no man to look after you."

"Men aren't worth the trouble," she grumbled beneath her breath.

Tom straightened his shoulders and preened like a barnyard cock. "That's 'cause you ain't crossed paths with a good one."

There were no *good ones*. Besides, Kat believed in the three-strike rule. First, Kat's father had never been in the picture. Second, Dwayne had bailed on her and Ricky. Third, Seth, who'd decided he wasn't cut out to be a daddy to someone else's kid after being in a relationship with her for almost a year, announced one morning out of the blue that he'd hired on with an oil rig off the coast of Louisiana. An hour later he was gone, leaving Ricky devastated. Three strikes—Kat was out of the ball game. She'd rather go it alone than suffer the heartache of another man disappointing her and her son.

Changing the subject, she said, "I need an Easy Soaker." The one she'd used on Tiger's hoof yesterday had torn.

"Should be one right there." Tom pointed to the boxes on the bottom shelf near the end of the aisle.

Kat checked. "Nope."

"Be right back." Tom set Kat's purchases on the counter and disappeared into the storeroom.

A few seconds later, the cowbell on the door jangled. "Well, lookie here. If it ain't our old boss."

Bracing herself, Kat faced the menacing ranch hands.

"Heard you hired that pretty boy to work for you." Roger stuffed a wad of chew between his gum and lower lip.

After Brody had settled into the trailer last night, she'd called Melissa's brother on his cell and explained the Roger-Clyde fiasco. She'd also informed Wes that Brody would be helping out for a while. Wes must have mentioned the incident to another cowboy in the area. News traveled fast through the Hill Country. Kat hoped none of the neighboring ranch owners leaked the news to the Bakers while they were in Europe.

Kat attempted to step past the men, but they intercepted her. She managed a scowl even though her stomach churned. "Really?" she said. "We're going to play this game?"

Right then the storeroom door opened and Tom walked out. "Got your Easy Soaker right here, Katarina." Tom stopped short when he became aware of Clyde and Roger. He cast an anxious glance at Kat. "Mornin', fellas."

"Yer doin' business with a traitor, Wheeler, you know that?" Roger's lip curled in disdain.

"Well, now times are tough, fellas. I treat everyone's dollar the same."

Roger turned and walked out, Clyde trailing like a devoted hound dog.

"What did they want?" Tom asked.

"Nothing." The bullies had a lot to learn if they

believed she'd tuck tail and run from a few snide remarks and evil glares. "What do I owe you for today?"

Tom rang up Kat's purchases and charged them to the Wild Rose account. She signed the ledger, then grabbed the shopping bag and left the store.

Halfway down the sidewalk Kat heard her name. "Mrs. Sovo! Mrs. Sovo!" People believed because she was the mother of a teenager she'd been married. Kat didn't recognize the blond-haired woman rushing toward her.

"I'm Beth Hunter. Ricky's told me a lot about you."

Confused, Kat said, "I'm sorry. Have we met before?"

The woman cleared her throat. "I took for granted that Ricky had mentioned Stevie."

Stevie? "I'm afraid not." Feeling inept, Kat fumbled for an excuse. "I've been really busy at the Wild Rose and I'm afraid I haven't had a chance to sit down with Ricky and ask what's new in his life." Kat nearly groaned at how that sounded.

"I'd forgotten that Mark and Melissa left on their trip." Beth sighed. "A European vacation sounds romantic, doesn't it?"

Having little experience with genuine romance, Kat kept her opinion to herself.

"Ricky invited Stevie to visit him at the Wild Rose, but I told him to check with you first."

Embarrassed but not shocked that Ricky hadn't mentioned his new friend, Kat asked, "How did the kids meet?"

"Booger's Bait Shop."

Kat knew of the bait stand, but was furious that Ricky

was sneaking off in the afternoons to meet his friend instead of doing homework.

"Ricky stopped at Booger's one afternoon when Stevie was buying bait and they got to talking about their favorite fishing holes. My husband, Karl, and I own ten acres south of Booger's. We have a spring-fed pond and Karl keeps it stocked with smallmouth bass. The kids love fishing there."

"I see." Kat didn't see at all.

Beth waved a hand in front of her face. "We don't have any horses, so when Stevie discovered that Ricky lived at the Wild Rose…" Beth cleared her throat. "But if you're too busy…"

"Too busy for what?"

"To give Stevie riding lessons. Ricky said you were really good with horses."

"I am good with horses, but I'm afraid my job at the Wild Rose leaves me with little spare time."

"Oh, goodness, I understand." Beth's cheeks turned pink.

Kat was ashamed of her rude behavior and blamed Clyde and Roger for rattling her nerves. She should be thrilled that Ricky had made a friend. "Why don't you drop Stevie off at the ranch for a riding lesson next Sunday." She'd find an hour in her day to give her son's friend a few pointers.

"Great! Thanks so much, Mrs. Sovo."

"Kat, please. Ricky's father and I never married." Kat couldn't care less what people thought of her. If they had the misfortune of meeting Dwayne they'd understand why there was no Mrs. in front of Sovo.

Needing to get back to the ranch Kat said, "Nice to meet you, Beth."

"Likewise. See you next Sunday."

Kat hopped into her truck and left town. Ricky had a lot to answer for when she got home.

Home. She and Ricky had lived at the ranch a few short months but already the place felt like home. No way would she allow Roger and Clyde to sabotage her and her son's dream of putting down roots at the Wild Rose.

BRODY STARED AT THE John Deere used to mow hay. Kat had left the ranch a half hour ago and he'd yet to drive the tractor from the barn. On occasion he'd operated a rotary mower when he'd worked for the Black Stone Ranch in Montana. This green monster had two large front tires and four massive rear tires. The modern piece of farm machinery had more bells and whistles than a pinball machine.

Ricky entered the equipment barn. "What's wrong? You look scared."

"I'm not scared." Brody didn't dare confess that he'd never handled a powerful machine like this before. "I was waiting for you."

"Why? Am I supposed to help?"

"Yep." Brody could use the extra moral support. Heck, he'd never been this nervous climbing on the back of a two-thousand-pound bull. *That's because the only thing you risk breaking is your neck.* If he ruined the expensive tractor, Kat would suffer the consequences. "Guess I'd better familiarize myself with the controls." He climbed into the cab and Ricky got in on the other side.

"Mom said the mower's out by the field."

Attaching the mower to the tractor was the least of Brody's worries. First, he had to get this beast out of the barn.

The cab of the tractor was nicer than the interior of Brody's truck—leather operator seat, a cup holder large enough to fit a quart-size water jug and a CD changer. Brody checked the four floor pedals. The one on the far left was the clutch. The two pedals on the right were the brakes—one for the left rear wheel and the other for the right rear wheel. The remaining pedal was the foot throttle used to control the speed of the tractor.

With a turn of the key, the engine rumbled to life. The instrument panel verified that the tire pressure was good, the gas tank full and the fluid levels for the oil and radiator normal. Brody released the clutch while he pressed the gas pedal and the tractor moved forward. The instant he cleared the barn, he engaged both brakes.

"The field's that way." Ricky pointed out the windshield.

"Find some music," Brody said as he drove away from the ranch yard.

Ricky fiddled with the dials, stopping when a George Strait song came on. "Mom loves this dude."

Brody got the tractor speed up to twenty miles per hour and it wasn't long before he spotted the mower attachment lying at the entrance to the field. Several attempts later, Brody managed to position the tractor in front of the mower. The mower cut standing hay and laid it in long, thin piles to dry out. A different attachment raked the hay into narrower rows for the baler to handle.

"I want you to stay out of the cab until I get this mower hitched."

"Why?"

Because Brody didn't want to risk either of them getting hurt if Ricky accidentally shifted a gear and the tractor moved. "Do as I say, kid, or I'll send you back to the barn."

"Sheesh, you're grumpy." Ricky jumped down from the cab and walked several yards away. A few minutes later he hollered, "What's taking so long?"

"Hold your horses." Brody double-checked the three-point hitch. Satisfied it appeared in working order, he secured the mower. Brody would have to remain alert in the driver's seat—constantly looking ahead to keep the tractor lined up with the rows and then glancing back at frequent intervals to make sure the mower didn't become clogged.

"Okay, get in," Brody said. Once Ricky was settled, Brody located the power takeoff shaft, which transferred the engine power to the mower, then cranked the engine. He set the tractor to the proper rpm and drove forward, lowering the mower at the same time. He circled the perimeter of the field until he found enough room to turn the tractor and mower on the headlands.

"Are you gonna start in the middle?" Ricky asked.

"Yep." Brody drove down the center of the field, mowing straight paths back and forth, trying to keep the rows as close together as possible to save on fuel.

If Kat's prediction of rain by the end of the week

came true, the crop would need to be removed from the field before then to avoid mold contamination. Brody glanced at Ricky. The teen looked bored to death. "Keep track of the time it takes to cut one row."

At the end of the row Ricky announced, "Three minutes."

"Six minutes up and back. How many trips do you guess we'll make before the field's cut?"

Ricky stared out the windshield, eyes scanning the sea of hay in front of the tractor. "I don't know. A hundred maybe."

"Okay, how long will it take to cut the entire field?"

"I need something to write on." Ricky rummaged through the cab until he found a pen and a piece of scrap paper. A few minutes later he pronounced, "It's gonna take us ten hours."

The dashboard clock read 9:00 a.m. which meant Brody would have to work in the dark to finish the field. "You're pretty smart."

"I know. My mom's good at math and she helps me if I get stuck on the problems in my workbook."

They drove in silence, Ricky keeping an eye on the mower in case it became clogged. "Hey, Brody?"

"Yeah?"

"You got a girlfriend?"

"Nope."

"What are those girls called again that hang out at all the rodeos?"

"Buckle bunnies." Brody had had his share of female attention since his divorce but he steered clear of entanglements. At the end of the evening, he left the bars alone.

"My dad said cowboys only rodeo 'cause they wanna a buckle bunny for a girlfriend."

"I reckon there are a few cowboys whose goal is to score with a hot buckle bunny." A busted leg usually put an end to the poor sap's career and love life.

"Is it true that most of them have long blond hair and big—" Ricky bounced his hands in front of his chest "—boobs?"

Talk about buckle bunnies abruptly ended when the front right tire hit a hole and the tractor pitched sideways, propelling Ricky into Brody's side. Knocked off balance, Brody slammed his feet against the brake pedals. The sudden stop threw Ricky forward and he smacked his forehead against the windshield.

"You okay?" Brody put the tractor into Neutral and set the emergency brake, then crouched in front of Ricky, who sat in a daze on the floor. He shook the teen's shoulders. "Say something, kid."

"Ouch." Ricky rubbed the red bump forming on his forehead. "What happened?"

"The tire hit a rut. Stay here." Brody climbed down from the cab, unhitched the mower, then returned to the driver's seat. "I'm taking you to your mom so she can look at that bump on your forehead."

Before Brody left the field, he saw Kat's pickup heading in their direction. "Never mind." He shut down the tractor engine. "Your mom's here."

Heart beating faster than a construction worker's jackhammer, Brody waited for Kat to park the pickup.

As soon as she opened the door, he said, "You need to take Ricky to the doctor."

"What happened?" Kat rushed to her son, who leaned against the front tractor tire, his face pale.

"I'm okay," Ricky said. "Brody's making a big deal out of nothing."

"The tractor ran into a hole and jolted sideways. Ricky hit his head against the windshield."

Kat swept her son's hair off his forehead and studied the injury.

"A doctor should check him over and rule out a concussion." Shoving his hands into his jean pockets, Brody paced.

"Honey, get in the pickup," Kat said.

"Awe, man. This sucks." Ricky did as he was told, slamming the truck door.

"Ricky's fine, Brody. It's just a bump."

"He could be seriously hurt."

Brody was practically a stranger yet he worried about Ricky's well-being more than Dwayne ever had. "He'll be fine." Kat retrieved the cooler she'd brought and set it at Brody's feet. "Drinks and food. If you get tired of mowing, I'll take a turn at the wheel." She handed him a walkie-talkie from her back pocket. "Hit the yellow button and I'll know you're ready for a break."

Kat returned to the pickup, then sped off.

"Why'd Brody get so upset, Mom? My forehead doesn't even hurt anymore."

"He feels bad that you were injured." Kat changed the subject. "I ran into Beth Hunter in town. She said you and Stevie are good friends and that you two hang out at Booger's Bait Shop." More silence. "Why are you sneaking off to Booger's without telling me?"

"I didn't say anything 'cause you wouldn't have let me go."

Exasperated, she argued, "Booger's is more than two miles away."

"I take the shortcut through the shallow part of the stream."

The stream Ricky referred to was located on the far side of the ranch. With Roger and Clyde threatening to stir up trouble, she didn't want her son caught alone on the property. "You tell me if you want to go to Booger's or visit Stevie and I'll drive you."

"You don't care if Stevie and I hang out?"

"Not as long as you finish your chores and keep up with your homework. As a matter of fact Mrs. Hunter is dropping Stevie off at the ranch next Sunday for a riding lesson."

"Really?"

Kat chuckled. "Really."

"Cool, Mom, thanks."

Ricky's enthusiasm melted Kat's heart. Her son's smiles had been few and far between since he'd blamed her for Dwayne's absence. She parked the truck in the ranch yard. "I could use your help in the barn."

"Okay."

No protest? "You sure you didn't hit your head harder than you think?"

"Nah. I'm good." Ricky got out of the pickup, took two steps, then fainted.

BRODY ALIGNED THE TRACTOR with the barn doors, then backed the machine into its proper spot and cut the engine. He closed his eyes, willing the tension to drain from his body. He'd been worried sick about Ricky since the accident. Kat had shown up shortly after supper time to relieve him, but he'd ignored her and mowed the entire field himself, thanks to a set of powerful headlights. Eager to see that the kid was okay, Brody walked straight to the foreman's cabin. He thumped his fist twice against the door.

Kat greeted him with a smile. "I kept a plate warming in the oven for you." She stepped aside. "I hope you don't mind leftover Mexican casserole."

"Where's Ricky?" Brody asked.

"In his room."

He followed Kat into the kitchen. "Did you take him to the doctor?"

"Actually the doctor stopped by the ranch."

"He's okay, right?"

"Ricky has a mild concussion."

The blood drained from Brody's head and he grabbed the edge of the countertop to steady himself. "Concussion?"

"Ricky fainted after we returned to the cabin this afternoon, so I phoned Dr. Helman. She said as long as he takes it easy for a couple of weeks he should be fine."

The pressure building inside Brody's chest cut off the air to his lungs and he wheezed. "Why didn't you mention his concussion when you stopped by the field earlier?"

"You waved me off before I had a chance to hop out of the truck."

"I never meant for Ricky to get hurt."

"Of course you didn't." Kat removed a foil-covered plate from the oven and set it on the table. "Iced tea?"

"Sure."

She poured two glasses of tea and set them on the table, then pulled out a chair and sat. Brody ate, not tasting the food.

"I bumped into Clyde and Roger at the feed store today."

"Doesn't surprise me." Brody suspected the disgruntled ranch hands hadn't moved on.

Kat's cell phone rang before he had an opportunity to ask if the two men had spouted any threats.

"Kat speaking." Her shoulders stiffened. "Be right there." She snapped the cell phone shut.

"What's wrong?"

"That was Wes." Kat left the table and threw on a jacket. "There's smoke coming from the hay field you just mowed."

Smoke meant fire. Had Clyde and Roger spied on Brody today, then set fire to the hay while he'd driven the tractor to the barn? He shoved his chair back and stood.

"Finish your supper. I can handle this." Kat shut the door in Brody's face.

Damn it! He followed Kat outside. No way was she going out alone in the dark. Brody had slipped up today with Ricky, but he was determined to protect Kat from whatever danger awaited in the hay field.

Chapter Five

Brody slid onto the front seat of the truck and Kat stomped on the accelerator. She'd been embarrassingly naive to believe Clyde and Roger were all talk and no guts. Kat peeked at Brody and winced at his solemn expression.

"Go ahead and say it."

"Say what?" he asked.

"I told you so." He'd warned her that Clyde and Roger meant trouble, but she'd believed his reaction had bordered on melodrama.

"Never mind that. I hope the damage is minimal."

There was no minimal—not when any loss of the expensive crop would reflect badly on Kat. The ride to the field took forever, Brody's stiff posture sending off signals that he'd rather be anywhere else than in her truck. His cagey demeanor didn't surprise her.

Brody was a restless soul. A man on the move. He lived out of his truck and spent his days traveling from rodeo to rodeo, never remaining in one place long enough to hang up his hat. Sure he'd agreed to work at the Wild Rose until the Bakers returned, but Kat wasn't banking on him to keep that promise. Her past relationships with men had taught her to rely on herself and no one else. For now, she'd count her blessings that Brody was present to lend his support.

She slowed the truck and turned onto a dirt path, breathing a sigh of relief that the night sky wasn't glowing orange. Up ahead, Wes's truck lights illuminated the section of smoldering hay. The veteran ranch hand was in the process of creating a break line in the row. Kat parked her pickup next to Wes's and left the lights on. She retrieved two rakes from the truck bed, tossing one to Brody.

They fell in alongside Wes and raked the singed hay into a pile between two rows. In no time flat the three of them had separated the smoldering grass from the rest of the crop.

"We're lucky," Kat said, wiping sweat from her brow. "It could have been worse."

"Whoever did this, didn't intend to burn the whole field," Wes said.

Kat caught a whiff of the ranch hand's beer breath. "How'd you discover the fire?"

"Smelled smoke in the air after I left the Ice House."

Wes must have chugged a couple of beers on the way home from Consuelo's Ice House and decided to take the shortcut through the ranch, which led past the hay field. Thank goodness he hadn't finished off a twelve-pack or he might not have detected anything amiss.

"Wes, this is Brody Murphy." Kat introduced the two men. "He mowed the field today."

The men shook hands. "Any guesses on what was used to ignite the hay?" Brody asked.

"Gasoline. There's an empty gas can at the edge of the field."

"Clyde and Roger want to scare me into hiring them back," Kat said.

Wes leaned heavily on his rake. "Then hire 'em back."

"So they can sit on their bums and do nothing? I don't have time to babysit them."

"I've got all I can handle moving the horses in the pastures now that we're shorthanded." Wes turned his attention to Brody. "Heard you're gonna hang around for a while."

"Looks that way."

"Well, we're done here." Wes tipped his hat, then got into his truck and drove off, leaving Kat alone with Brody, who stared at her as if she'd lost her mind.

"What?"

"Those low-down snakes couldn't care less if they're caught causing trouble." Brody stared at her. "You know what else?"

Kat shook her head, thinking Brody looked mighty sexy all fired up.

"They know damn well you won't go to the authorities, because your job is on the line. You're at their mercy, don't you see?"

She did see. But Kat refused to be bullied. She was tired of living in a trailer. Tired of setting up shop for a few days, then having to pack her things and move on to the next ranch. "I can't live like you, Brody."

"What are you talking about?"

"A gypsy lifestyle." She perched her hands on her hips. "It's been three years since Ricky and I have had a chance to call any place home. I'm not giving in without a fight."

"Why don't you park the trailer somewhere permanent and make people bring their horses to you?"

"It's not that easy. The Bakers have a top-notch facility here and I have the best equipment available to me, which makes my job a lot easier and more enjoyable."

"So this is all about you?" Brody pointed an accusing finger at Kat.

How dare he insinuate she was selfish? "Who are you to criticize? You put yourself first every day. You travel wherever you want, do whatever you want and answer to no one."

"Precisely, Kat. I have no one to answer to anymore."

Anymore? "What do you mean?"

"Forget it." Brody tossed his rake into the truck bed.

Good grief. The man could at least finish an argument. They returned to the foreman's cabin in silence and without a word Brody walked to the trailer.

"Want me to heat up a second plate of leftovers for you?" Kat called after him. The trailer door slammed shut on her question.

Moody cowboy. Determined to forget Brody's rudeness, she checked on Spot in the barn. The old dog was fast asleep on his bed near the supply room. She freshened his water bowl before leaving the barn. Halfway to the cabin she saw headlights on the ranch road. A visitor this late at night meant one thing—trouble.

The loud rumble of a busted muffler echoed through

the air as the pickup squealed to a stop in the yard. The driver stepped from the cab.

Aw, shit. "What are you doing here, Dwayne?"

"That ain't a very polite greeting." Ricky's father sneered. The years had been kind to Dwayne—because he'd spent most of them sitting on his ass. Tall, broad-shouldered with dark hair, he looked ten years younger than his thirty-five. Too bad his pretty face camouflaged a rotten inside.

"I stopped by to visit Ricky."

"The festival in Bandera was yesterday."

"Something came up."

A woman most likely.

"Didn't think Ricky would care if he missed the thing."

He cares, you dope. "Where'd you get the wheels?" The last time Dwayne had shown up he'd hitched a ride.

"A friend."

"Why don't you hightail it back to your *friend's*." The squeak of the trailer door caught Kat's attention, but she kept her eyes on Dwayne. He crowded her space, and Kat retreated a step. Dwayne had never abused her—she simply didn't like craning her neck to speak to him. "It's late and Ricky's not feeling well."

"What's wrong with him?"

"He's got a mild concussion."

"How'd that happen?"

As if you care. "He lost his balance in the tractor and hit his head against the windshield."

Dwayne chuckled. "Got his big feet all tangled up, did he?"

Kat bit the inside of her cheek to keep from cursing. When would her son realize he was better off without this man in his life? It amazed her that Ricky couldn't see his father for who he really was—a schmuck.

"Guess I'll bunk down in the trailer." Dwayne made a move to pass Kat, but she held up a hand.

"You can't sleep in the trailer."

"Why not? You and Ricky are using the cabin, aren't you?" Dwayne had visited the Wild Rose shortly after she and Ricky had settled into the small home. She'd been lucky he'd only stayed a couple of days before he'd gotten bored and moved on.

"A guest is using the trailer."

"You got a new lover, Kat?"

"That's enough, Dwayne. He's a hired hand."

"The hell you say. Fire him and hire me. I could use the money."

Dwayne could always use the money. Much to her shame, the only way she could coax him to vamoose when he overstayed his welcome was to bribe him with money. "If you're determined to hang around, then sleep in the barn."

"I'm Ricky's father. I deserve better than the barn."

Brody appeared out of nowhere. A good four inches shorter than Dwayne, Brody had to tilt his head to make eye contact. "Is there a problem, Kat?"

"No. I was telling Dwayne where he could sleep tonight."

"Who the hell are you?" Dwayne asked.

"The hired help."

"Good. Grab my gear from the truck bed and put

it in the trailer, then take your stuff to the barn," Dwayne said.

"Sorry, no can do." Brody clenched his hands into fists. "If you want to settle this another way…"

Dwayne's mouth sagged and Kat pressed her fingers to her lips to keep from laughing. In order to preserve his handsome face, Dwayne avoided brawls. Obviously Brody had no qualms about marring his good looks.

"Never mind." Dwayne faced Kat. "Count me in for breakfast." He grabbed his bedroll from the pickup then disappeared inside the equipment barn.

"You okay?" Brody asked.

"Sure."

"So he's Ricky's father?"

"In the flesh."

"He won't try anything stupid tonight, will he?"

"No."

"I'll cover for Ricky tomorrow and muck out the stalls before breakfast."

Dwayne would never do that for his son. "Thanks, Brody." If Dwayne stuck around long enough the hired hand might teach him a few things about work ethic.

Then again maybe not. Some men just couldn't be counted on for anything.

BRODY ENTERED THE FOREMAN'S cabin at 7:00 a.m. Monday morning, expecting to find Ricky's father seated at the kitchen table eating breakfast. The room was empty.

"Hey, Brody," Ricky greeted from the hallway.

The teen appeared healthy, but head injuries were tricky. "Shouldn't you be resting in bed?"

"I'm fine. Mom says I can do most everything but ride my dirt bike and horses." His shoulders sagged. "And visit Stevie."

"Who's Stevie?" Brody asked.

"A friend. Stevie's coming next Sunday and Mom's gonna—"

"Give Stevie a riding lesson." Kat waltzed into the kitchen, her dark hair secured in a ponytail that swished across her shoulders. She wore jeans and a long-sleeved blouse. Taken as a whole the outfit was nothing special, but Brody studied each article of clothing separately and found plenty to admire.

The jeans Kat wore hugged her fanny like a second skin, the denim worn white along the seams. Kat had tucked her pink shirt into the jeans and a brown leather belt with a giant-size silver buckle emphasized her small waist. She'd rolled the shirtsleeves up to her elbows, showing off her creamy, tanned skin. When she reached into the cupboard above the stove, the shirt tightened across her generous breasts. Kat was one sexy lady and Brody felt a sudden urge to find out if she was as good a kisser as she'd been in his dreams the previous night.

"Hungry?" Kat asked.

The one-word question triggered a flashback of Brody's midnight fantasy. He and Kat had put out the fire in the hay field then had celebrated with a kiss. One moment they were making out on the ground, the next they were soaping each other in the shower.

"Brody, are you all right?" Kat's brow furrowed.

"I'm not much of a talker until I drink my first cup of coffee."

"Ricky, fetch Brody his coffee while I put breakfast on the table."

"Need any help?" Brody asked.

"No, thanks. Pancakes and sausage are already warming in the oven." After delivering the food to the table and pouring the orange juice Kat sat down and nudged Ricky's elbow off the tabletop. "Your father arrived last night."

Ricky's eyes lit up. "He's here?"

"Yes."

"Where?"

"He bunked down in the barn."

If Ricky thought it odd that his father had to sleep in the barn he didn't comment. "What's Dad want to do today?" Ricky popped a sausage link into his mouth.

"I don't know, but remember Dr. Helman said nothing strenuous."

"Maybe Dad'll play video games with me." Ricky turned to Brody. "The Bakers hooked up an Xbox to the TV in my room."

"That was nice of them," Brody said.

"I'm gonna play 'Call of Duty' until Dad wakes up." Ricky inhaled his food then carried his plate to the sink before disappearing into his bedroom.

"What's the matter?" Brody asked when he caught Kat playing with the food on her plate.

"Nothing. Why?"

"You seem upset. Did Ricky's father bother you last night?"

"No. I just hate that Dwayne shows up out of the blue." Kat set her fork aside. "Ricky expects to have an exciting time with his dad then nothing goes as planned.

In the end I'm left with a heartbroken teenager who blames me for forcing his father to hit the road."

"Do you?" Brody asked.

"Do I what?"

"Force your ex to leave?"

"Dwayne's not my ex. We never married. And yes, when I reach my breaking point, I kick him out."

Brody poured himself a second cup of coffee, then topped off Kat's mug. "How long does he usually hang around?"

"Only a day or two, but this time he'll stay longer."

"Why's that?"

"Not why...*who*." She sighed. "Dwayne won't leave, because you're here."

Mind your own business. Eventually Brody would move on and never see Kat or Ricky again.

"Dwayne doesn't want me, but he doesn't want anyone else to have me, either."

Whoa. Hang on here. "I don't have you."

Kat raised her hands in the air. "I know that, but Dwayne doesn't."

"And you want him to assume there's something going on between us?"

"He'll do that all on his own." Kat narrowed her gaze on Brody. "Would it bother you if Dwayne thought we were a couple?"

Yes. No. Maybe.

Although he'd sworn off relationships since his divorce, Brody admired Kat for her strength and independence. She didn't need or want a man to take care of her and Ricky. No matter how tempting, becoming involved with Kat was out of the question. Brody had been alone for so long he'd forgotten what it felt like to be part of a couple or even a family.

Been there. Done that. Failed miserably.

Dodging Kat's question, he asked, "Ricky's dad should be paying child support. Have you taken him to court?"

"In all the years I've known Dwayne, he's only held down one job that brought in a steady paycheck—a fork-lift operator at a home-improvement store. He'd worked there less than a year before he quit."

"How does he support himself?"

"He works odd jobs or lives off friends."

Brody had never lived off friends but he did hire himself out for odd jobs to earn money for his entry fees. He wasn't much of an improvement over deadbeat Dwayne. "Mind if I ask why you two never married?"

"After I became pregnant my grandfather confronted Dwayne and insisted he marry me, but Dwayne refused." She thrust her chin in the air. "I was an embarrass-ment to my grandparents, but they didn't turn me out. In hindsight I'm glad Dwayne and I didn't marry. He's a worthless father and provider."

When Brody and Kelly had divorced, she'd filed the paperwork and her parents had paid for the lawyer and court costs. Kelly had asked for nothing from Brody except that he never try to get in touch with her. She'd considered him worthless, too.

Kat dumped her remaining coffee down the drain. "The hay needs to be raked and baled before rain moves in on Friday."

"Want me to start today?" Brody asked.

"No, the piles need to dry out. Wednesday you can

rake the hay and Thursday you can bale it." She nodded to the telephone. "The Montgomerys called this morning and asked if I'd run out to their ranch and fix a shoe that's bothering one of their horses. They're good friends with the Bakers so I agreed to help."

"Besides mucking stalls is there anything else that needs to be done?"

"I'd appreciate you keeping an eye on Ricky. I don't want him leaving the ranch with Dwayne."

Brody hadn't signed on to be Ricky's protector. His offer to help with ranch chores was becoming more complicated by the minute. "Thanks for breakfast." He left the cabin before Kat begged another favor from him. Brody threw himself into mucking stalls, hoping the strenuous labor would block out the voice in his head warning him to quit asking questions and to butt out of Kat's and Ricky's personal lives. His plan succeeded until Ricky entered the barn midmorning.

"Hey, Brody. Do you think my dad's gonna wake up soon?" The kid had waited all morning for his father to roll out of bed.

The last thing Brody wanted to do was confront good ol' Dwayne, but Ricky deserved better even if his father couldn't be bothered about spending time with him. "Wait here." Anger spurred Brody's steps across the ranch yard.

Dwayne's snoring greeted Brody when he entered the equipment barn. A six-pack of empty beer cans were strewn about the ground. *Lazy-ass drunk.*

Quiet as a mouse, Brody climbed into the tractor and cranked the engine. Dwayne flew out of his makeshift bed on top of the hay bales and stood in a daze.

Brody cut the engine and climbed down from the tractor cab. "Morin'."

"What the hell did you do that for?"

"Checking to see if the tractor starts."

Dwayne glared. "I was sleeping."

"Ricky's been waiting all morning for you to wake up."

"So what." Dwayne shoved his fingers through his hair.

The man was an idiot. "Your son wants to spend time with you."

"Boy's a pain in the backside. He ought to be able to entertain himself."

"He wants to show you his new Xbox game." Brody clenched his hands into fists and resisted the urge to slug the man.

"You sure are gettin' cozy with my son. You just as cozy with his mom?"

"That's none of your business."

A bark of laughter erupted from Dwayne's mouth. "Having a kid together gives me certain rights."

Arrogant bastard. "That's not how Kat sees things."

"So it's that way between you and her, huh?"

Brody opened his mouth to deny any relationship with Kat but decided not to waste his breath. Dwayne would see things how Dwayne wanted to.

"Hey, Dad, you're up." Ricky stopped inside the barn and gaped at the two male adults. "What's wrong?"

"Nothing," Brody said, schooling his expression. "Your father and I were discussing ranch business."

"You wanna play a video game, Dad? I've got this—"

"I need to speak to your mother."

"She's gone," Ricky said.

"What time will she be back?"

Ricky looked at Brody.

"Kat didn't say." Brody nodded to Dwayne. "Ricky's waiting for your answer."

"Answer to what?"

"Do you wanna play Xbox?" Ricky said.

"Yeah, sure. Wait for me in the cabin." Ricky dashed from the barn then Dwayne faced off with Brody. "Keep your nose out of my business with Kat and Ricky."

Brody hoped to do exactly that but worried he was fighting a losing battle. "Make sure you don't keep Ricky waiting." Brody stopped at the barn door. "You might want to pick up after yourself. Kat doesn't like messes."

As far as messes went, Dwayne was a big one, but Brody wasn't much better.

Chapter Six

"Hang on, boy." Kat adjusted the Easy Soaker boot on Tiger's hoof, early Friday morning, then waited for the gelding to put weight on his leg. Her patient refused. Exasperated, she pulled up a stool and massaged his fetlock joint, hoping to coax him into cooperating.

The barn was quiet. The local weatherman had been correct for a change and the rain he'd predicted by the end of the week had arrived after midnight. A light drizzle continued to fall, but Kat welcomed the moisture now that the hay had been baled and safely stored in the equipment barn.

"C'mon, Tiger. Give it a try." She coaxed his hoof deeper into the solution of warm water, Epsom salt and Betadine. Kat had babied the hoof with medicated soaks and poultices, but the healing process was slow going.

"Having trouble with Tiger?"

Kat jumped inside her skin and spun on the stool.

Brody. How long had he been spying on her?

"He's acting like a typical male," she said.

"How's that?"

"Stubborn."

The corner of Brody's mouth quivered. "Be a good

boy, Tiger." Brody grabbed a soft brush from the grooming kit hanging on the stall door and cleaned the horse's coat in long, even strokes. Tiger responded to the pampering by putting weight on his injured hoof.

"You have the magic touch," Kat whispered. They worked in silence—Brody brushing, Kat massaging. From her seat on the stool, she studied Brody's muscular thighs visible beneath the gelding's belly. Her face heated when she pictured his strong legs squeezing the sides of a bull.

"How long have you been rodeoing?" she asked.

"I've competed on and off through the years for fun, but I became serious about the sport two years ago."

"Do you have brothers or sisters who rodeo?" So far Brody had been tight-lipped about his personal life.

"I don't have any family left."

The odd note in his voice caught Kat's attention and she stopped rubbing Tiger's leg. "Tell me about your folks."

"I was an only child and my parents were up there in years when they had me," Brody said.

"How long ago did they pass away?"

"I can't remember off the top of my head, but it was before I married."

Married? Kat sucked in a quiet breath. The day she'd convinced Brody to stay on at the ranch, he'd denied that he had a wife or girlfriend waiting for him in Lubbock. "Where's your wife now?"

"Ex-wife. She moved to California after our divorce."

Kat hated prying but..." How long have you been divorced?"

"A little over two years."

During the past week Kat had asked Brody a few personal questions, hoping he'd share his past with her. She wasn't sure why he was willing to talk now, but fearing he'd clam up any second she bombarded him with more questions.

"What was her name?"

"Kelly."

"We're you high school sweethearts?"

"No. I met Kelly right after I graduated." He chuckled. "She was stranded on the side of the highway with a flat tire. I changed her tire and in lieu of payment, I asked her out on a date. She said yes."

"How old were you when you married?"

"Twenty."

"That's young."

"So is having a baby at seventeen."

Touché. "Don't think I didn't get crap about that from my grandparents."

"How did your parents react?" Brody asked.

"They weren't in the picture. My mom ended up pregnant with me at fifteen, but had no idea which of her boyfriends had fathered me. My grandparents raised me from birth and my mother ended up dead at seventeen from a methamphetamine overdose."

"I'm sorry."

Kat shrugged. "To tell you the truth I never missed having a mother. My grandparents were the best people in the world and I'm glad Ricky had the chance to know them before they died." Kat was somewhat of a private person but she'd happily share her life story if it kept Brody in the barn a while longer.

Since Dwayne had arrived at the ranch, Brody had stopped taking his meals with her and Ricky. Kat was stuck listening to Dwayne's obnoxious tall tales at the dinner table. Ricky, bless his heart, hadn't discovered the real reason his father remained with them longer than usual—Kat refused to pay him to leave.

"I know I thanked you already, but I'm grateful to you for bringing in the hay crop." Wednesday, Brody had raked hay, then yesterday he'd run the baler through the field and stacked the hay bales in the barn all by himself.

"Glad I was able to help."

The first thing Kat did each morning when she woke was peek out the front window to see if Brody's truck remained parked in the yard. He'd confessed himself that he wasn't any good at staying in one place very long. Even though Kat hoped Brody would work for her until the Bakers returned in May, she wasn't counting on it.

Brody brushed Tiger's rump, then his haunch and across the girth until he stood next to Kat. The heat from his thigh felt as though it seared the side of her face.

"There's a rodeo in San Marcos a week from tomorrow. I'll muck out the horses stalls in the morning before I take off."

If Brody was mentioning the rodeo, then he intended to remain at the Wild Rose at least another week. Time would tell if she'd misjudged him. "I wish I could go along and watch you ride," she said.

Brody chuckled. "No, you don't."

"Why not?" Kat stood and set the stool aside.

"I stink at bull riding."

Startled by his honesty, she asked, "Then why do you rodeo?"

"Keeps me on the move."

"I guessed right."

Brody's gaze caressed Kat's face. "Guessed right about what?"

"You're a runner." She raised a hand. "Not that it's a bad thing to roam from town to town." But it sure wasn't what Kat wanted for her and her son. Her dream was to remain in one place long enough to make memories.

Brody tugged a strand of hair that had escaped Kat's ponytail. "You're right about the running part." The quiet admission pulled at her heartstrings.

Drawn by the swirling emotion in Brody's dark eyes, Kat leaned closer. How long had it been since she'd kissed a man? *Forever.* Brody's gaze settled on her mouth and her pulse quickened.

"Don't," he whispered.

"Don't what?"

"Don't want me to kiss you."

"I don't." They both knew she was lying.

Brody lowered his head. Kat lifted her face. At the last second she considered turning away, then his breath caressed her lips and she nixed the idea. His mouth settled against hers. His scent—a mixture of soap, aftershave and damp leather—surrounded her. She tunneled her fingers through his hair, knocking his hat to the ground. He deepened the kiss, sweeping his tongue inside her mouth.

She felt the first tingle in her toes then the tickling sensation moved to her breasts. A moan worked its way up her throat and escaped her mouth.

"Figured you were sleeping with the boss."

Brody broke off the kiss and Kat teetered on her boot heels. *What rotten timing.* "What do you want, Dwayne?"

"For starters, some of what you're handing out for free."

In a quick move, Brody snatched Dwayne's shirt collar and backed him up against an empty stall door. "Watch how you speak to the lady."

Dwayne shoved away from Brody. "Since when have you been a lady, Kat?"

"Knock it off, Dwayne." She crossed her arms, hoping to hide her thundering heart. "Did you come in here to say goodbye?"

"Hey, haven't I spent quality time with Ricky this week?"

Quality time—yeah, right. Ricky did his school lessons in the afternoons while Dwayne napped on the sofa.

Needing a moment to gather her composure, Kat turned her back on both men and removed Tiger's soaking boot. She dried the hoof with a clean towel then slathered a medicated poultice on the abscess. After covering the area with gauze pads she enclosed the hoof in a small-size infant diaper, which she secured with a layer of vet-wrap followed by duct tape. Satisfied the wound would stay clean she led Tiger into his stall, then faced Brody and Dwayne. Both men were locked in a stare-down.

"Get out of my way. I've got work to do." Kat stomped out of the barn. Damn Dwayne for interrupting the most romantic kiss she'd ever experienced. And damn Brody for awakening her sensual side—a romantic tryst was the last thing she needed in her life right now.

Or was it?

"SHE'S A HOT LITTLE NUMBER, ain't she?" Dwayne said after Kat left.

Ignoring the jerk, Brody packed the grooming brush away then turned to leave. Dwayne blocked his exit.

Brody resisted punching the jerk in the nose. Pretty face aside, what had Kat seen in this guy? *Don't be too quick to judge. Dwayne might be the biggest loser on the planet, but he didn't cost a child her life.*

"Kat's holding out longer than usual." Dwayne poked his finger at Brody's chest. "Because of you."

"What are you talking about?"

"Listen close. This is how it works. I show up unannounced, get in the way and generally irritate Kat until she gets sick of me."

Jerk. "Then what?"

"Then she pays me to get out of her hair." Dwayne shoved his extra height in Brody's face. "You told her not to give me any money, didn't you?"

"Kat's a smart girl. She doesn't need me or anyone else to advise her how to handle leeches."

"You sure talk big, for such a puny guy, don't you?"

Brody shoved Dwayne with such force the man stumbled and banged his shoulder against the edge of the barn door. "You don't scare me, cowboy. You're nothing compared to the two-thousand-pound bulls I wrestle each weekend." Brody left out the fact that most times he ended up with his face planted in the dirt. "Kat wants you gone, so hit the road."

"You're the hired hand. You don't get any say in how things go down between me and Kat." Dwayne straightened his shirt. "Ricky's my kid, not yours. You stay the hell out of my way." A minute later Brody heard a muffler backfire and the crunch of spewing gravel as Dwayne sped off.

Real smooth, Brody. What had gotten into him— standing up for Kat and Ricky? But Dwayne's indifference toward Ricky had rubbed Brody the wrong way. Ricky was alive and well. No matter how Dwayne had screwed up in the past, the man had an opportunity to make amends to his son. Brody would give anything for a second chance to be a better father to Angel.

He pushed the wheelbarrow to the far end of the barn then led a horse named Belle from her stall and hitched her to the center post. He grabbed the shovel and began mucking.

If he expected his mind not to stray, then he'd sorely misjudged his cognitive abilities. He couldn't stop replaying the kiss he and Kat had shared. Her taste lingered on his lips and he could still feel the way her soft mouth molded to his.... *Damn.* He hadn't been interested in a woman since his split with Kelly. Why now?

Better yet, why Kat?

Maybe if you'd indulged in an occasional one-night stand with a buckle bunny your testosterone levels wouldn't be off the charts. There was a valid reason Kat's kiss had blown him away—he was sex-starved. He hadn't been intimate with a woman since his divorce.

No matter what excuse he offered, Brody didn't dare

become involved with Kat. She was the kind of woman who held a man accountable for his actions. No way in hell Brody could live up to her expectations nor did he want to. He'd failed one woman in his lifetime. He refused to fail another—especially one on the road to making a better life for her son.

"HEY, KAT?"

Kat counted to ten in her head before answering Dwayne. Following his and Brody's confrontation in the barn last Friday, she'd spent the week devising ways to get rid of Dwayne. The scumbag had thwarted all her efforts, so she'd decided to simply throw him out. "What?"

Dwayne walked into the kitchen scratching his bare chest. "Where's my clean laundry?"

Kat nodded to the duffel bag propped against the cabin door. Dwayne's boots rested on the floor by the bag and his coat, hat and truck keys sat on top.

"What's that supposed to mean?"

"You're leaving." She kept her voice down, aware of Ricky watching TV in his bedroom down the hall.

"Is this some kind of April Fools' joke?"

"Nope." Dwayne had been at the Wild Rose as long as Brody—approximately two weeks. But unlike Brody, Dwayne had worn out his welcome.

"What if I don't want—"

Kat held out a bank draft from her checkbook. She hated that she'd given in to him.

He read the check then laughed. "You must want me gone real bad."

"Throw on a shirt, say goodbye to Ricky then leave."

"Gettin' kind of stingy." He fluttered the check in front of Kat's face. "You're lucky you got a good job."

"If you don't want the money, give it back."

Dwayne yanked the check out of Kat's reach. "What about Ricky? We had plans next week."

This was the first she'd heard of any *plans*. "If you want more time with your son, hire a lawyer and file for joint custody."

"That's cold." Dwayne pulled a shirt from the duffel and slipped it on. He gestured to the oven where a tuna fish casserole baked. "You could feed me before I—"

"You're leaving, Dad?" Ricky walked into the room.

"Your mom says it's time for me to go." Dwayne sent Kat a nasty glare.

"But—"

"Until next time, Ricky." Dwayne saluted.

It was wishful thinking on Kat's part, but she hoped there wouldn't be a next time.

"Can I come with you?" Ricky followed Dwayne outside.

"I got no way to take care of you."

"I can take care of myself. Let me come, please, Dad."

Kat stood in the doorway, silently cursing Dwayne. He couldn't even look his son in the eye.

"I got things to do. You'll just be in the way. Besides, you got your schoolwork."

"I can do my homework in the truck while you're driving."

Dwayne put his hand on Ricky's shoulder and pushed him away from the driver's side door. "This isn't my truck. Now go on. Your mom—" Dwayne's eyes pleaded with Kat for help. After he realized she wasn't coming to his rescue, he said, "Your mom needs you more."

Dwayne threw his duffel into the front seat, then revved the engine and drove off without a honk. The ass hadn't even given his son a hug goodbye.

Kat braced herself as Ricky walked back to the cabin. Instead of throwing a tantrum he asked in a subdued voice, "Is Brody gonna eat with us now?"

"I don't know. If he's hungry he'll show up when I ring the bell."

Evidently Brody wasn't hungry, because Kat and Ricky ate alone. She attempted to fill the silence with questions about the history lesson Ricky had completed in his workbook, but after several one-word responses she gave up. Kat cleared the dishes from the table and Ricky took a small bowl of tuna fish casserole out to the barn for Spot. Another hour passed and no Brody, so Kat fixed a plate for him.

Brody opened the trailer door on the fourth knock. "Hi," Kat said. His face in the shadows, she couldn't read his expression. Their kiss had happened seven days, thirteen hours and eight minutes ago—but who was counting? Ever since the kiss, Brody had acted polite but cool toward Kat. "I hope you like tuna fish."

"Hey, Brody!" Ricky sprinted across the drive. "You wanna hang out?"

"You know how to play poker?" Brody asked.

"No."

"I'll teach you." Brody opened the screen door, took

the dinner plate from Kat's hand then ushered Ricky inside. The door shut in her face.

"You're welcome," Kat muttered.

"Mom said you're going to a rodeo in San Marcos tomorrow. Is that your gear?" Ricky pointed to the canvas bag on the floor by the recliner.

"Yep."

"Where's the rest of your stuff?" Ricky's gaze shot around the trailer.

"I don't have much else." Except a few pairs of jeans and shirts. And Angel. He had a framed photo of his daughter—the only one Kelly had allowed him to keep. He sat at the table and dug into the casserole Kat had brought him. "Your mom's a good cook."

"I know. Do you have an iPod?"

"Nope."

"Then what do you do while you're driving to all your rodeos?"

"Watch the road."

"Real funny. Do you play games on your cell phone?"

"I don't carry a cell phone." The fewer connections he had to people the better.

"What do you do if you get bored?"

"Ponder life." Brody had dissected his life all the way back to grade school and had yet to come up with an explanation as to why he'd fallen into the habit of putting himself first before those he loved.

"You ever go to the movies?"

"No." The last movie theater Brody had sat in was five years ago when he'd taken Angel to see a Disney cartoon. Brody expected the kid to fire off another question but Ricky clammed up, his gaze dropping to the Formica tabletop. "Something on your mind?" Brody asked.

"My dad."

"What about him?"

"Mom kicked him out today." Ricky expelled a deep breath. "I think she gets mad that Dad and I have fun together."

"So you enjoy hanging out with your dad?"

"Yeah." Pause. "Sometimes."

Brody hated to see the teenager hurting. Dwayne had a great kid but chose to ignore Ricky most of the time. Brody flinched at the criticism. He was no winner in the father department, either. "Have you asked your dad why he doesn't show up more often?"

"No."

"How come?"

Ricky picked at his nails. "I'm afraid."

"Of what?"

"If I bug him he won't want to see me again."

Ricky was damned if he did and damned if he didn't. No kid should have to feel like an obligation or inconvenience. Brody would always be grateful that Angel had been too young to realize he'd put his needs ahead of hers. He'd loved his daughter, but he'd allowed his work to take precedence over family, justifying his choices to ease his conscience.

He remembered bargaining with God on the way to the hospital. If He would save Angel, then Brody would take the job at the meat processing plant and give up his cowboy ways. But God hadn't listened. Brody had gambled and lost everything—his daughter, his marriage and his position at the Black Stone Ranch.

"I heard Dad tell Mom she shouldn't be stingy with her money 'cause she's lucky she's got a good job."

"Luck has nothing to do with your mom's job. She's worked hard to become a respected farrier. I bet when things get tough, your mother doesn't give up. I'm not saying you two haven't had struggles, but it's because of your mother's determination that she's been able to take good care of you."

"After my great-grandpa died, it was hard, 'cause we didn't have anyone to help us."

There was a part of Brody that yearned to make up for the past and be the man Kat and Ricky turned to in difficult times. But mother and son deserved better than him. "So you want to learn how to play poker?"

Ricky's eyes lit up. "Sure." He rummaged through the drawer next to the sink and found a deck of cards. Time passed in a blur until a knock sounded on the door. Brody eyed the clock—ten-thirty. "Sorry, kid. Looks like you missed your curfew." Brody braced himself when he opened the door. Kat stood on the steps, her hesitant smile drawing his attention to her mouth. Would he ever be able to look at Kat and not remember their kiss?

"We're not finished with our card game," Ricky grumbled.

"Doctor Helman's coming tomorrow to check on you. She'll know if you're not getting enough rest."

"But I'm going to go to the rodeo with Brody?" Ricky's gaze pleaded. "Right, Brody?"

Put on the spot, Brody wasn't sure how to respond.

Kat rescued him. "Dr. Helman has to give you a clean bill of health before Stevie can visit."

"But—"

"We had to cancel Stevie's lesson because you hit your head. You don't want to make your friend wait another whole week, do you?"

"Yeah, okay." Ricky put the cards back in the drawer. "Thanks for teaching me how to play poker, Brody."

The minute the boy was out of earshot, Brody asked, "Has Wes spotted any trouble on the other side of the ranch lately?"

"No. Everything's fine."

"Those guys aren't finished with the Wild Rose, so keep your guard up tomorrow while I'm gone." Brody was certain Clyde and Roger were lying low, waiting for the right opportunity to strike again.

"When will you be back?" Kat asked.

"Late. Don't count on me for supper."

"Oh, here." She pulled a wad of bills from her jean pocket. "Payday. I thought you'd want cash since you wouldn't have time to stop at a bank before heading out of town."

"Thanks." Damn. His gaze kept straying to her lips.

"Well, good luck tomorrow."

He didn't want her to leave. "You shouldn't have caved in and paid Ricky's father to go away."

"I know, but I have bigger worries than Dwayne right now."

God help him, he wanted to kiss her.

"Bring home the buckle, cowboy."

Brody watched Kat return to the cabin, wishing

with all his heart that somewhere along his travels he'd stumble upon redemption. Peace. Forgiveness.

Maybe in his next lifetime.

Chapter Seven

Kat patted Tiger's rump and led him from the barn to the paddock. "There you go, boy." She shut the gate and waited. The gelding didn't budge. "Move, Tiger." Frustrated the horse refused to put weight on his healing hoof, she fetched Clementine from her stall and put the mare in the corral with Tiger.

Clementine was a feisty horse and Kat hoped she'd coax Tiger into playing with her. The mare didn't let her down. Clementine charged Tiger, turning at the last second, her tail swatting his face. Tiger bolted and the two horses ran the length of the enclosure. Problem solved, Kat returned to the cabin.

She was miffed that Brody had left for San Marcos before she'd crawled out of bed this morning. She shouldn't care that he hadn't bothered to say goodbye, but she did. Never mind that they'd shared a kiss and traded personal information about their families, Kat had come to respect Brody for his strong work ethic and his kindness toward Ricky. She'd thought they were becoming friends.

Maybe it was just as well he hadn't waited to say goodbye. Friendship was fine, but that's where Kat drew the line with Brody. She'd fought long and hard to become self-sufficient, and roaming cowboys were nothing but heartaches in the making. The next guy she became involved with would have roots sprouting from the bottom of his boots.

Determined to forget Brody, Kat entered the cabin, expecting to find Ricky at the kitchen table doing homework. The room was empty. He'd probably stayed in bed this morning, still angry about their heated argument last night. Kat was ashamed she'd lost her cool with Ricky, but wished her son would take off his blinders and see his father for who he really was—a man who only cared about himself.

"Why did you kick Dad out?" Ricky had shouted.

"Because."

"Why don't you want me to have a dad?"

"Dwayne doesn't act like a father."

"Yes, he does!"

"Then how come he rarely visits you? How come he doesn't call you every few days? How come he doesn't take you places?" Her questions had brought tears to Ricky's eyes.

"'Dad can't be here all the time 'cause he's busy."

"Doing what? He doesn't have a job, Ricky. He's never paid a penny of child support since you were born."

"So. You take care of me. We don't need his money."

That her son had defended Dwayne so fiercely had hurt Kat. Couldn't Ricky at least have acknowledged her efforts to provide for him and all the sacrifices she'd made through the years?

"It hasn't been easy keeping a roof over our heads and food on the table since Grandpa died."

"You're just jealous 'cause Dad doesn't love you."

"Your father never loved me—not even in the beginning when we dated."

"Then how come you had me?"

"Because I was young and stupid and I believed..." The rest of Kat's words had trailed off when Ricky's stunned look registered in her brain. Silence loud enough to shatter her eardrums had filled the cabin for all of three seconds before Ricky fled to his bedroom and slammed the door.

"Ricky? Honey, I'm sorry. I didn't mean what I said." She'd stood in the hallway for a half hour begging his forgiveness. Ricky had refused to open the door. Kat had spent the night in her bed tossing, turning, crying and cursing.

Enough sulking. "Rise 'n' shine, Ricky!" she hollered down the hallway. No answer. "Hey, you awake?" She thumped her knuckles against the bedroom door. "I'm coming in."

The room was empty. The bed neatly made.

Kat's stomach plummeted. *Not again, Ricky.* Praying he hadn't run off, Kat went outside and rang the supper bell. No Ricky. She checked the equipment barn and storage sheds. The Bakers' ATVs were parked in their original spots as was Ricky's dirt bike. If he left the ranch, he'd left on foot.

"Don't do this to me, Ricky. Not today." Had he run off in search of Dwayne or had he decided to pay Stevie a visit? Before she drove to the Hunter's, Kat returned to Ricky's bedroom in hopes of finding a clue as to his whereabouts.

She tore apart the bed. Nothing. She peeked beneath the mattress. Oh, dear—girlie magazine. When had her son become enthralled by the female body? Better yet, what kind of mother didn't notice her son was growing up right under her nose?

A moment later Kat's cell phone rang.

"Hello."

"Kat, this is Sue Montgomery. Guess who I found walking along the side of the road?"

"My son, I hope." Kat sank onto the bed and willed her heart to stop pounding.

"Ricky says he's heading to San Marcos to watch a bull rider compete today."

Her son had gone after Brody not Dwayne. Kat left the bedroom, grabbing the truck keys on her way out of the cabin. "Where are you?"

"Almost to the Wild Rose."

"I'll be right there." Five minutes later Kat stopped at the entrance to the ranch. Ricky stood outside Sue's car, leaning against the passenger door—hands shoved into his jean pockets. Face scowling.

Relieved her son appeared fine, but angry that he'd scared ten years off her life, Kat slammed the door harder than she'd meant to. She sent Ricky a sober look. "Get in the truck." Kat stuck her head through the passenger-side window of Sue's car. "Thanks for bringing him home. I owe you one."

"Everything okay between you two?"

"Yes. No." Kat closed her eyes. "We got into an argument about Ricky's father last night."

"Say no more." Sue's understanding was both a relief and an embarrassment. Kat had been shoeing horses in the area long enough for most folks to have met or heard about Ricky's deadbeat dad.

"Thanks again, Sue."

"Anytime." Sue tooted the horn then drove off.

As much as Kat wanted to hug Ricky and apologize for their argument yesterday, she resisted as she slid into the driver's seat. "What part of our never-hitchhike-again discussion didn't you understand?"

No response. "If I take you back to the cabin you'll just up and leave again when my guard's down." Ricky remained mute. Kat sighed, feeling like a cornered animal with only one way out—straight into the trap. She shifted into Reverse and drove back to the cabin. "Wait here."

"Why?"

Guilt prompted her spur-of-the-moment decision. "I've got to fetch my purse. We're going to the rodeo."

Ricky's sullen expression evaporated. "Really?"

"Yes, really." Inside the cabin Kat called Wes and Dr. Helman's office to inform them that she and Ricky would be gone for the day. San Marcos was an hour and a half from Bandera. Once Brody finished his ride she and Ricky would hurry back to the Wild Rose.

Kat and Ricky arrived at the San Marcos rodeo grounds at noon. The event was small compared to most competitions and parking was free. Kat paid her and Ricky's admission fee then they weaved through the milling spectators.

"Look, Mom. There's Brody." Ricky took off before

Kat could stop him, leaving her no choice but to follow.

She lost sight of Ricky after he dashed behind the grandstands, but managed to find her way to the stock pens where Ricky stood among a group of jawing cowboys.

One of the men caught sight of her and spoke to the others. The group moved on, leaving Ricky and Brody behind. Brody tipped his hat. "This is a surprise."

"We came to watch your ride then we have to get back to the ranch," Kat said. With Clyde and Roger on the loose, she was nervous about being away from the Wild Rose too long.

"Brody, can I stay with you when Mom leaves?" Ricky's eyes pleaded.

What if Brody had plans to meet a girlfriend later? Or maybe he hoped to get lucky with a buckle bunny. Imagining Brody with another woman made Kat's stomach cramp. *Knock it off. One kiss doesn't give you any claim to the man. Or so she told herself.*

"Brody might have other plans," Kat said.

"I don't. Ricky can hang out with me today," Brody said.

"Are you sure? You might want to catch up with friends later."

"Quit trying to talk Brody out of letting me stay, Mom." Ricky glared at Kat. "I know you don't like Dad, but I thought you liked Brody."

"I do like Brody." Heat suffused Kat's cheeks. "But—"

"Ricky, things aren't always what they seem," Brody said.

Kat appreciated Brody's efforts to defend her but Dwayne's rejection had hurt Ricky deeply and he needed someone to blame. Kat had done her best to protect her son's innocence and keep his hope alive that one day his father would make him a priority in his life. Had the time arrived to be honest with her son? Was Ricky old enough to handle the truth?

"Honey, your father stayed as long as he did this time because I refused to pay him to leave," Kat said.

"I don't get it."

"Your father loves you—" *in his own pathetic way* "—but he only visits us if he's low on cash."

"How much did you give Dad?"

"Two hundred dollars."

"Dad said you were stingy with your money but two hundred dollars is a lot."

"Yes, it is."

"What does Dad do with the money?"

Drink. Pay for sex. "I don't know."

"How come Dad doesn't get a job?"

Tell him the truth. "Your father would rather live off of others than hold down a steady job."

"Is that why he says I can't live with him—'cause he doesn't have a steady job?"

A lump formed in Kat's throat. One day she hoped her son would realize how much she loved him and that he was better off with her. "That's one reason. He also doesn't have his own place to live."

"Can't he get a stupid trailer like we have?"

Ouch. Ricky made their home sound cheap. Kat had done her best to make the trailer cozy, but obviously her son was old enough to see it for what it was—a trashy metal box on wheels.

Ricky stabbed the toe of his boot against the ground. "So because Dad's lazy and doesn't want to work I'm stuck living with you?"

"Ricky…" Brody scowled.

"You live with me because you're my son. I love you and I want what's best for you."

"What if what's best for me is not living with you?"

Kat clenched her hands until her nails bit into her palms. The pain was nothing compared to the excruciating agony clawing at her heart. "As soon as you turn eighteen and graduate from high school you're free to go off on your own."

Ricky faced Brody. "If you had a kid you'd get a job so you could take care of him, wouldn't you?"

The blood drained from Brody's face and his eyes glazed over.

Worried, Kat said, "Don't drag Brody into this, Ricky." When Brody continued to stare into space, Kat dug a five-dollar bill from her pocket. "Get us each a hot dog and find a place to sit. I'll meet you there in a minute." Ricky took off toward the concession stands.

"I'm sorry you were put in an awkward position." Kat hoped an apology was enough. Obviously Ricky had touched a nerve in Brody.

"He's a good kid." Brody's voice sounded rusty.

"I know. I just wish he had a decent male role model."

"I'm not qualified to be a role model, Kat." Brody refused to make eye contact.

"No one's asking you to. Ricky and I have been on our own for a while now." If truth be told, Kat wanted more from life than a secure job and a decent home for her and Ricky. She wanted a real family. Ricky needed a father. She needed a husband—a man to share her problems with. To support her dreams. To hold her at night while she slept.

A tiny part of Kat wished Brody wasn't on the run. His heated looks made her pulse race. Her body temperature spike. Her skin tingle. Yes, she was attracted to Brody. He was sexy, good-looking, hardworking and downright nice. But anything more than friendship between them spelled trouble for her heart.

"I'd better go," Brody said. "Bull poker's about to start." He walked off without a backward glance.

Bull poker? Kat made her way to the stands and located Ricky near the top of the bleachers. "Thanks," she said when he handed her a hot dog.

"Ladies and gents, it's time for our bull-poker event!"

The crowd stomped on the bleachers creating an impressive din.

"I thought Brody was riding a bull," Ricky said.

"Guess he's doing this instead." Maybe he had a better chance of earning prize money in bull poker. "There he is." Kat pointed to where Brody waited with three other cowboys for a turn to sit at the plastic card table and chairs in the middle of the arena.

"Folks, we've got four certifiably insane cowboys signed up for this event. The winner collects five-hundred bucks!"

Brody adjusted his protective vest and decided the

announcer was right—he was insane. He'd left the Wild Rose before dawn, determined to forget about Kat and Ricky for the day, but the only thing he'd forgotten was his bull rope in the trailer. Sure, he could have borrowed another competitor's equipment, but he'd still lose the event. Instead, he'd joined the cowboys-without-brains club and signed up for poker.

Now here he was about to make a fool of himself in front of a woman he couldn't get off his mind. He studied the bull that had been picked for the poker game—Big Ben. Brody waited for his adrenaline to kick in but his thoughts were wrapped up in Katarina Sovo.

His attraction to Kat was inconvenient at best and his growing need to be there for Ricky was something Brody couldn't explain and didn't care to acknowledge.

"Okay, cowboys, pick your seats at the poker table!"

Brody trailed the men into the arena. Lucky him—he ended up with his back to the bull chute. He scanned the stands until he caught sight of Ricky and Kat. Ricky gave the thumbs-up sign and Kat clasped her hands beneath her chin as if praying. If Brody wasn't careful he could get used to being fussed over.

"Folks, let me introduce you to four ignoramuses." The fans hooted. "We got Jeremy Rhodes from Austin." The man waved his hat. "Pete Crosby from Boerne." Pete fist-pumped the air. "Wade Fellerman from right here in San Marcos." The cowboy earned a standing ovation. "And the lucky son of a gun with his blindside to the bull is Brody Murphy from…" The announcer paused then chuckled. "From somewhere in Montana."

Brody hadn't bothered to include his hometown on the signup sheet because it wasn't home anymore.

"Cowboys, keep your hands on the table at all times. The last man seated wins!"

The chute door opened. Brody held his breath as Big Ben charged the table. The bull veered to the right at the last second, but not before the local cowboy had ditched his seat. Big Ben skidded to a stop, turned and pawed the dirt.

"We got three cowboys left, folks! Get ready, 'cause Big Ben's gonna dig a few graves!"

The bull charged the table, his horn clipping one cowboy's shoulder and sending him flying out of his chair. The man scrambled to his feet and made a dash for the rails.

"Well, folks. Now we know who the dumbest two of the group are—Brody Murphy and Pete Crosby!"

Big Ben pawed the dirt and snorted. A rodeo clown jumped into the arena and danced about, trying to rile the bull. It worked. Big Ben charged. Brody prayed the bull would turn at the last second. Fat chance.

The bull rammed the table, sending it and Crosby airborne. Brody managed to cling to his chair, but as the bull pivoted away, it stomped Brody's left boot. The pain was excruciating for all of ten seconds then his foot went numb. Damn bull had probably broken his toes.

At least he'd won.

"There you have it folks—the world's dumbest cowboy is five hundred bucks richer!"

The pickup men guided Big Ben to the stock pen and Brody limped out of the arena.

"Hey, Brody, that was awesome!" Ricky raced toward him. Kat wasn't far behind.

"Are you all right?" Her pretty face scrunched with worry.

"Bruised foot." For an instant, Brody relished Kat's concern then just as quickly shut the door on the emotion.

"Maybe you should have your foot checked out by a—"

"I'm fine, Kat." Brody collected his money, then he and Ricky walked Kat to her truck in the parking lot.

"Don't cook tonight. We'll grab supper on the way home," Brody said.

Home—he'd meant the Wild Rose. As he watched Kat drive away, pain stronger than the ache in his throbbing foot tweaked Brody's chest. He blamed it on indigestion.

"C'MON IN."

Kat entered the trailer shortly before 10:00 p.m. Saturday night. "I brought an ice pack for your foot and pain medication."

"Thanks." Brody placed the ice on the kitchen table, then hobbled to the cupboard, filled a glass with water and popped a few pills into his mouth.

"Ricky said you stopped for pizza on the way home."

"That kid has some appetite. Good thing the place was an all-you-can-eat buffet."

Brody sat down in the recliner and she motioned to his boot. "Let me see your foot."

"It's nothing." Translation—he couldn't get his boot off.

Kat knelt in front of the chair and tugged on the boot, but the leather wouldn't budge. Stubborn man should have removed his boot right after the bull had stepped on his toes.

"Let me." Brody cursed but managed to free his foot. He peeled the sock away, and Kat grimaced at the black-and-blue marks across the top of his swollen foot.

"Your big toe was spared." The other four were probably broken. She grabbed the step stool from the kitchen and a pillow from the love seat, then elevated Brody's foot and placed the bag of ice on his puffy toes. "You'd better keep off your feet tomorrow, and—"

"Mooch off of you like Dwayne did?"

"You wouldn't know the meaning of the word *mooch* if it hit you in the back of the head." She adjusted the ice bag when it threatened to slide off his foot. "You work hard for every penny you earn." Brody continued to glare and Kat worried there was more to his bad mood than a few broken toes.

"What's the matter, besides your sore foot?" she asked.

"You. You're the matter."

Startled, Kat pointed to herself. "Me? What have I done?"

"Never mind."

"Don't sulk. Tell me what's got your drawers all twisted in a knot."

Brody sat straighter in the chair. "You're justifying your actions—telling yourself that giving Dwayne money to disappear is okay, when it's not."

"What I do with my money is none of your—"

"It is my business, Kat, because I've been in your shoes. I've put my needs and wants first—"

"Stop." Kat held up a hand. "I paid Dwayne to leave for Ricky's sake. Not mine."

"Sooner or later you have to quit giving in to Dwayne or you'll teach Ricky that in order to get what he wants he just has to hold out long enough."

"What's wrong with holding out?" she asked.

"I held out and lost everything that mattered most to me."

Brody's haunted eyes startled Kat. His pain was so real she ached to hug him. Before she made the worst mistake of her life, Kat bolted from the trailer.

Chapter Eight

Kat set the pitchfork aside and closed the latch on the horse stall, then collapsed on a hay bale. She'd run out of energy. Brody's late-night confession had robbed her of precious sleep.

I held out and lost everything that mattered most to me.

What had Brody lost? He'd been married...was he still in love with his ex-wife? If he was, why should it matter to her?

It matters because you care about Brody as a friend.

Kat feared her feelings for Brody were edging beyond friendship. It wouldn't take much on Brody's part to coax her into caring deeply for him. Despite the hay fire, Dwayne's stressful visit and suffering broken toes, Brody had kept his promise to help her out at the Wild Rose. Most men would have had enough and moved on.

Brody had stayed.

To be honest, Kat had expected Brody to be long gone by now. Maybe he wasn't a runner so much as a man on the move until he found whatever he was searching for.

He's not searching for you, so don't get any ideas about the two of—

"Stevie's here, Mom!" Ricky's shout cut off the sarcastic voice in her head. She checked her watch. 11:00 a.m. Where had the morning gone? Pasting a welcoming smile on her face, Kat stepped from the barn and froze.

Stevie was a *girl*.

Surprised by Stevie's gender, Kat wasn't sure how to react. First, the girlie magazine beneath her son's mattress and now discovering his best friend was female. Panic exploded inside Kat. How many times had Ricky sneaked off to be alone with Stevie? Kat had never had the birds-and-the-bees talk with her son. That was Dwayne's job. She should have known better than to hand over the responsibility to a man who'd insisted a girl couldn't get pregnant the first time she had sex.

Beth Hunter stood with her daughter next to the corral. Kat walked in their direction, sending a silent message to Ricky—why didn't you tell me Stevie was a girl? He avoided her gaze. Smart boy.

"Hello, Beth."

"Kat." Beth introduced the young girl. "This is my daughter, Stevie."

The petite blonde held out her hand. "Nice to meet you, Ms. Sovo."

"Same here, Stevie." Kat watched Ricky shift nervously from one foot to the other. He should be worried after keeping this a secret from her. "I hear you like horses."

"Yes, ma'am." The teen's blue eyes flashed toward Ricky before she returned her attention to Kat. "Ricky says you're the best with horses. And he said his great-grandfather used to be a horse whisperer."

"That's true. My grandfather and I have always had a special bond with horses. Have you ridden before?"

"Once."

Beth jumped into the conversation. "A long time ago Stevie rode a pony at a traveling carnival. For some reason the animal spooked and bucked. Stevie fell off and broke her arm and hasn't ridden a horse since."

"But I'm ready to try again," Stevie said.

"We'll take things slowly. It's important that you aren't afraid of the horse. When animals sense human fear, they become nervous."

"What time would you like me to fetch Stevie this afternoon?" Beth asked.

"Why doesn't she stay for supper, then I'll drop her off before dark," Kat said.

"Okay then." Beth turned to her daughter. "Mind Ms. Sovo."

"I will, Mom."

"C'mon." Kat led the way to the barn, resisting the urge to peek over her shoulder to see if the teens were holding hands. "I have the perfect horse for you to get to know."

"Her name's Sweet Pea," Ricky said when Kat stopped outside the mare's stall. "She's really old."

"How old?" Stevie asked.

"Twenty-two." Kat patted the mare's neck. Sweet Pea's breeding days had long passed her by, but because she was well mannered and affectionate, the Bakers had kept her as a personal pet. "Here's how you let Sweet Pea catch your scent." Kat blew her breath up the horse's nose and the mare whinnied.

Stevie giggled then squeezed her eyes shut and puffed at Sweet Pea's face.

"She likes you," Ricky said.

The heated look that passed between the teens warned Kat that it wouldn't be long before looks turned into touches and then... She knew kids experimented with sex at an early age these days, but thirteen was too early. "Ricky, show Stevie where we keep the horse treats and bring a few out here for Sweet Pea."

"Sure."

Kat watched the kids disappear inside the storage room. A few seconds passed then she heard laughter. When the two returned, Stevie's cheeks were a shade pinker. Kat presumed the two had kissed.

"This is how you feed a treat to a horse." Ricky set the biscuit on his palm. Sweet Pea used her lips to nuzzle the treat into her mouth.

Kat backed the kids up, then led the mare from her stall and tied her to the grooming post in the center of the barn. She placed a stool several feet away. "Stevie, you sit here." Kat handed her son the grooming belt. "Ricky, you demonstrate how each brush and comb is used and in what order. I'll be back in a few minutes then Stevie can groom Sweet Pea."

Kat hurried from the barn and made a beeline for the trailer. She hadn't seen Brody all day—not that she'd expected to since she'd insisted he rest his foot. She hated to disturb him, but if she didn't vent about this latest situation with Ricky, her head would implode. She banged on the door.

"Come in!"

She stepped inside, shut the door and gasped. "Oh, my God!"

"Is it Clyde and Roger?" Brody had his swollen foot halfway into his boot.

"No, no." She'd caught Brody's wince when he'd tried to tug on the boot. "You should have your foot x-rayed."

"A doctor can't do anything for broken toes."

He could prescribe a strong painkiller while the bones heal, but Kat didn't press her point. She predicted that, like Dwayne, Brody didn't carry health insurance and couldn't afford an E.R. visit.

"If it's not trouble with Clyde and Roger, then why are you upset?" Brody asked.

"Ricky's friend Stevie."

"What about him?"

"Her. Him is a her." Kat peered out the window toward the barn. "I can't believe Ricky didn't tell me that Stevie's a *girl*."

"Is this Ricky's first girlfriend?"

"Yes. No." Kat sighed. "I think so."

Brody grinned. "What's the problem with Stevie being a girl?"

"Everything. What if she ends up pregnant like I did the first time I had sex?"

"You got pregnant the first time you had sex?"

"Dwayne coaxed me into the backseat of his truck—" She frowned. "Never mind my past. I don't want Ricky to do that to a girl."

"Have you talked to him about sex?"

Kat's gaze settled on the door. "Dwayne was supposed to."

Brody didn't comment—he didn't have to. She knew what he thought of Dwayne.

"Talk to Ricky, Kat. Find out if he and Stevie are sexually active."

"I plan to." The talk couldn't come soon enough.

"Good. And don't forget to discuss birth control."

"I know."

"Be sure to ask Ricky if he knows how to use a condom."

Heat suffused Kat's face. Were mothers expected to buy a box of condoms and say "Here practice"? Kat's shoulders sagged. She didn't want her baby boy to grow up.

Brody limped across the room and clasped her shoulders. "Everything's going to be okay, Kat. Discussing sex with Ricky might be embarrassing, but he'll appreciate hearing the straight facts." He chuckled. "Take it from a guy who learned about the birds and the bees in the high school locker room."

"If he has any questions about...you know, guy things, can he talk to you?"

"Absolutely."

Kat's lips quivered. "And you'll tell him girls really like the guy to be a virgin on their wedding night?"

"No, but I'll tell him a guy should never sleep with a girl unless he has—" Brody stared into Kat's eyes "—feelings for her."

Kat had come to the trailer for moral support, not to be tempted into kissing Brody. "I'd better go," she whispered. She didn't want Ricky and Stevie out of her sight for more than a few minutes.

Kat was well aware that a few minutes was all it took to change one's life forever.

BRODY PAUSED OUTSIDE the door of the foreman's cabin and gathered his composure. No matter how he denied his feelings, the mother-and-son duo were working their way beneath his skin, tempting him to want more out of life than a bare existence.

Until he'd met Kat, he'd acknowledged his existence for what it was—empty. He'd accepted his solitary lifestyle, roaming from rodeo to rodeo. Aside from his buddy Drew, never connecting with anyone until Kat. She made him want more.

Deep down, Brody wanted forgiveness. He wanted someone to say… *You didn't mean to make bad choices. You didn't mean for Angel to suffer from your selfishness.* Brody feared that Kat was the one person who could break down his defenses and convince him that it was okay to lay the past to rest. Okay to be happy. To enjoy life. To live again.

He couldn't allow that to happen.

Brody lifted his hand to knock but the door suddenly opened and a petite blonde stood before him.

"Oh, hi. You must be Mr. Murphy. Ricky's mom just sent me to get you. I'm Stevie." The girl smiled, showing off silver braces with bright pink bands.

Heart hammering, Brody entered the cabin.

Stevie shut the door then returned to the kitchen, where Kat stood at the counter cutting fresh vegetables. Agony ripped through Brody's chest as he stared at

Ricky's friend. Would his Angel have looked similar to Stevie if she'd lived to be a teenager? Would his daughter have worn her long blond hair loose like this girl or in a braid as Angel had worn it the day she'd died?

Ricky joined Brody by the door. "She's hot, isn't she?" Brody scowled and Ricky's eyes widened. "What did I say?"

Watching the way Ricky ogled Stevie, reminded Brody of what he'd been like when his hormones had kicked into gear and he'd viewed girls in a new light.

"Supper's almost ready." Kat set a pan of lasagna on the table and Stevie followed with a basket of bread and a veggie plate. The water glasses had already been filled. Kat sat down and reached for Brody's plate.

"Aren't we going to say grace?" Stevie asked.

"Thanks for reminding us, Stevie." Kat elbowed her son. "Ricky, will you handle the prayer please?"

"Dear God, thanks for this food and thanks for Stevie."

Kat cleared her throat. "You mean her friendship, right?"

"Ahh...yeah."

Brody caught the way the teens couldn't take their eyes off each other and had a hunch the kids had already passed the hand-holding stage.

"Ms. Sovo, is it true that Ricky might be able to go to the junior high in Bandera next fall?" Stevie asked.

"I hope so," Kat said.

"We can join an after-school club together." Stevie spoke to Ricky.

"Maybe you'll be in some of the same classes," Kat interjected.

Ricky shook his head. "Stevie's really smart, Mom. She gets all A's and she's in the—" he glanced at Stevie. "—what's that program you're in?"

"Gifted and talented." Stevie smiled shyly.

"She wants to go to college and be a doctor," Ricky bragged.

"That's terrific," Kat said.

The rest of the meal passed in casual conversation. Brody learned that Stevie was an only child and her father managed one of the restaurants in Bandera. Her mother worked as a substitute teacher at the local elementary school and both sets of grandparents lived in Austin.

While Kat dished out ice cream for dessert, she asked, "How did you come by the nickname Stevie?"

"It's not a nickname. I was named after my grandma's favorite singer, Stevie Nicks." The teen wrinkled her nose. "I think she has a horrible voice."

"I like your name," Ricky said.

Stevie could have had a pimple the size of a walnut on her nose and Ricky would still have been enamored with the girl.

Kat checked the clock. "We'd better take Stevie home."

"Thanks for the horse lessons, Ms. Sovo."

"My pleasure, Stevie."

"We'll wait for you in the truck, Mom." Ricky bolted for the door.

"Nice to meet you, Mr. Murphy," Stevie said.

"Likewise."

The teens left and Brody cleared the table. Kat moved to the front window and peeked around the curtain.

"You're spying."

"Darn right, I am." Kat gasped.

Brody hurried to the window and stared over Kat's shoulder. He made it in time to see Ricky lean in and kiss Stevie.

"Oh, no." Kat rubbed her forehead.

"No big deal. Lots of teenagers kiss."

A moment later, Ricky's hand inched up the girl's waist.

Uh-oh.

Kat grabbed her jacket, then left the cabin, banging the door loudly behind her. The noise startled the teens and they jumped apart. Stevie scrambled into the truck. Ricky waited near the rear bumper.

"You did that on purpose, Mom," Ricky whispered as Kat approached. Checking first to see that both truck windows were shut, she answered, "Yes, I did."

"Teenagers kiss, you know."

"You were about to step over the line with Stevie."

"What line?"

Lord help her. "You were going to touch her breast."

Ricky's face flushed bright red. "So? I bet you've let guys touch your boobs."

"Don't be disrespectful, young man." Kat counted to ten while she reined in her emotions and gathered her thoughts. "I'm an adult, Ricky."

"So?"

"So you should only do things that are age appropriate."

"You think me and Stevie are having sex, don't you?" Ricky glared.

"Are you?"

"No."

Relief swept through Kat, leaving her light-headed. "Are you planning to?"

"I don't know." Ricky shrugged. "Sure, I guess."

So much for relief. "Is Stevie on board with your plans?"

"Huh?"

"Have you and Stevie talked about having sex? About who's going to take responsibility for using birth control? What you'll do if she gets pregnant?"

"Ahh…"

"You do know that having sex is how babies are made, don't you?"

"Duh."

"Then you know that Stevie is old enough to become pregnant if you two have unprotected sex. There's also the chance that one of you might catch a disease."

"You mean like AIDS?"

This really wasn't the time or place to discuss sex— not with Stevie waiting in the truck, but Kat feared if she postponed the talk until later Ricky would find excuses to avoid the subject.

"Well, there's that and other diseases like STDs."

"What are STDs?"

"Illnesses that stay in your body your whole life and they can be transmitted to every person you have sex with."

"Do you have diseases?" Ricky asked.

"No." *Thank goodness.*

"How do I keep from getting STDs?"

"You use protection."

"You mean like a hat?"

"Huh?"

"Jeez, Mom. A condom. You know, those things guy roll up their—"

"I know what a condom is, thank you." She just hadn't heard them called *hats* before. "And yes, wearing one protects you from all kinds of sexually transmitted diseases." Now for the million dollar question. "Have you ever used a condom before?"

"No, but they can't be that hard to figure out."

"You should practice a few times to make sure you don't tear a hole in it and risk getting the girl pregnant. The girl is trusting *you* to take care of her."

"Forget it." Ricky turned away, but Kat grabbed his arm.

"Sex is a serious thing, Ricky."

"I know. But you worry about the dumbest stuff."

"It's not dumb for a parent to want to prevent their child from following the same path they did."

"What do you mean?"

"Your father got me pregnant the first time we had sex."

"Really?"

"You and Stevie have your whole life ahead of you. Having a baby at your young age could interfere with Stevie's dream of going to college and becoming a doctor. A pregnancy at her age might also put her health at risk."

"Did I interfere with your dreams?" Ricky asked in a hushed whisper.

"You became my dream, honey." She cleared her throat. "But not all women feel that way about having a baby."

Ricky scuffed the toe of his sneaker against the ground. "So like, was dad your first?"

"Yes."

"How old was Dad?"

"Twenty." Old enough to know better than to have sex without a condom.

"Did Dad pressure you into having sex?"

"A little, but I was young and I thought I loved him."

"Did you like it?"

"Truth?"

Ricky nodded.

"Not really."

Ricky's eyes widened.

"I wasn't prepared for everything that would happen."

"Do you think I should wait to have sex?"

"I believe it would be a good idea for you and Stevie to wait a few years."

"But what if she doesn't like me in a few years?"

"Then you won't have wasted your first time on a girl who likes you one day and not the next." Kat brushed a lock of hair from Ricky's eyes. *Don't be in a rush to grow up, baby.* "Sometimes when a boy and girl have sex, the girl assumes the guy really loves her and that one day they'll get married."

"Did you think Dad would marry you?"

"I'd hoped your father would want to marry me after I became pregnant with you."

"But he didn't."

"No, he didn't."

The cab door opened and Stevie leaned out. "Umm…
are we leaving soon or…"

"We're leaving right now." Kat patted Ricky's shoulder then got in the truck. The drive to Stevie's was made
in silence as was the return trip to the Wild Rose. As
they pulled up to the cabin, Kat saw Dr. Helman's truck
parked near the barn. "Looks like Dr. Helman stopped
by to check on you."

She and Ricky walked down to the barn where the
doctor and Brody chatted.

"Hey, Dr. Helman," Ricky said.

"Howdy, Ricky."

Kat's gaze swung between the doctor and Brody. "I
see you've met Brody, Laura." She caught Brody's attention. "Laura's the only doctor who does house calls."

"So I've heard," Brody said.

Kat watched Laura's reaction to Brody but the tall,
big-boned, plain-faced doctor appeared immune to the
hot-looking bull rider.

"Hop up, Ricky." Laura lowered the tailgate on her
truck. She rummaged through her medical bag and removed a stethoscope and penlight, which she flashed in
Ricky's eyes. Two minutes later, she pronounced, "Good
as new. You can resume physical activity, but make sure
you wear a helmet if you ride a bike, ATV or a horse."

Ricky opened his mouth to protest, and Laura said,
"No exceptions, young man." She put away her instru-
ments and snapped the bag shut.

Kat nodded to Brody. "Laura, would you mind taking
a look at Brody's foot. He—"

"It's nothing, just a few bruised toes." Brody scowled.

"How'd you injure your foot?" Laura asked.

"A bull stepped on it," Ricky blurted. "Brody won at bull poker yesterday."

"Sit up here and take off your boot." Laura patted the tailgate.

Brody cooperated and Laura studied his big bare foot. The swelling appeared to have gone down some but the bruising was darker.

"Without an x-ray it's tough to say for sure, but if I had to guess I'd say the smaller toes are fractured, probably in more than one place." She removed a roll of medical tape and cotton batting from her bag then stuck the cotton between Brody's toes, before taping all four toes together. "Keep the wrap on for a week and continue to ice your foot."

"Thanks." Brody tugged on his sock.

"Do you have a pair of athletic shoes you can wear until the swelling goes down?" Laura asked.

"Nope."

"Then use this walking boot on your foot." Laura rummaged through the backseat of the truck until she found a navy blue sandal-like contraption with Velcro straps.

"That looks stupid," Ricky said after Brody had the sandal on.

"Thanks, kid." Brody reached for his wallet. "What do I owe you, Doc?"

"Nothing. First house call is free." She closed the tailgate once Brody slid off.

"I appreciate you coming by, Laura," Kat said.

"No problem. Nice to meet you, Brody."

"Likewise, Doc."

"How did things go?" Brody asked after Laura drove off.

"Don't worry," Ricky muttered. "I'm not gonna have sex with Stevie." He whistled between his teeth. "C'mon, Spot."

As soon as Ricky was out of earshot, Brody said, "Sounds like you two had a good talk."

"I don't know about good, but I covered the basics."

"Now that you started the conversation, Ricky will come to you if he has any questions."

Kat hoped so. "I was a little freaked out about the whole thing this afternoon and it was nice to have someone to talk to. So thank you."

"Hey, what are friends for, right?" Brody said.

"Right." Kat watched Brody hobble to the trailer, his swagger sexier than ever as he avoided putting weight on his injured foot.

All the talk about procreation put Kat's hormones in a tizzy. What she wouldn't give right this moment for a bout of steamy sex. Too bad the man she wanted to fool around with had just referred to himself as her friend.

Chapter Nine

Kat spied through the window Saturday night on Brody and her son. The males sat on the trailer steps deep in conversation. Two weeks had passed since her birds-and-the-bees talk with her son. When Ricky had asked to speak with Brody in private, she suspected he'd wanted Brody's advice on girls and dating. She wished Ricky had turned to her instead. Kat hated for him to become too attached to Brody—not when the bull rider had every intention of moving on.

Brody's stayed a month.

Each day that passed and Brody remained at the Wild Rose surprised and pleased Kat. She'd never admit it out loud, but with Clyde and Roger on the loose, she felt safer with a man living fifty yards from the cabin.

Not just any man—*Brody*.

Ricky wasn't the only one becoming attached to the cowboy.

Kat dismissed the thought. Aside from finding Brody sexually attractive, any affection she felt for him was solely based on gratitude for his help at the Wild Rose. *Yeah, right.* Maybe if she kept telling herself that she'd eventually believe it.

Right then Kat's cell phone rang. "Hey, Wes. What's up?" The news wasn't good. "I'm on my way."

She was out the door and across the drive before Brody's voice caught up with her.

"What's wrong?" He hurried toward her, his limp less pronounced. Yesterday, he'd finally managed to get his boot on over his injured foot without grimacing.

"That was Wes. Two of the horses got loose and are out on the road."

"I'll help." Ricky leaped from the top of the porch steps to the ground.

"Honey, I need you to stay here and keep an eye on the cabin."

Ricky swore.

"Young man..." Kat tossed her son a warning glare.

"Okay, I'll stay." He whistled for Spot. The dog trotted out of the barn and followed Ricky to the cabin.

"Back up the truck and I'll hook up the trailer," Brody said.

Kat did as he asked, then Brody secured the hitch and joined her in the front seat.

"Wes must have been driving along the fence line when he saw the horses," she said.

If Kat wasn't going to say it, Brody would. "My guess is that Roger and Clyde are behind this." The ranch hands had been in the back of Brody's mind all week. He'd had a hunch the two men had been biding their time, waiting for Kat's guard to drop.

A half mile south of the Wild Rose, Kat spotted Wes's truck and pulled onto the shoulder. The pickup's headlights illuminated the area and Brody saw that one of the horses had been caught and tied to the bumper of Wes's truck. The other gelding dodged the lariat Wes failed to throw properly.

"I'll help Wes while you load the other horse." Careful not to startle the skittish animal, Brody approached Wes. He noticed the trickle of blood that ran down the animal's foreleg. Better a flesh wound than a broken bone, which would have been disastrous for the horse and Kat.

"Need a hand?" he spoke in a hushed voice.

"Nope," Wes said.

Brody smelled beer on the man's breath. "You sure?"

Wes flung the rope at the horse's head and missed by a mile. Brody might stink at bull riding but years of working cattle had taught him how to lasso livestock. He made a move to retrieve the rope, but Wes snatched the lariat from the ground.

"Back off, Murphy. I got this." The rope smacked the horse across the nose.

Idiot.

The gelding spun toward the road and Brody leaped forward, preventing the animal's escape. Not until the horse settled down did Brody feel the pain in his foot resulting from his quick reflexes. He limped past Wes and growled, "My turn."

Brody clicked his tongue. The sound caught the horse's attention and the animal turned toward Brody. The rope sailed through the air and over the horse's head, settling low on its neck. The gelding didn't protest—the animal understood he was in good hands.

"That's how you lasso a horse," Brody muttered as he led the animal to the trailer.

"Let me check his leg before you load him." Kat inspected the animal's injury, then pronounced, "He doesn't need stitches, thank goodness." She nuzzled the gelding's neck. "Poor baby. You must have been scared to death out here." She moved aside and allowed Brody to coax the horse into the trailer.

He shut the door, then spoke to Wes. "Any idea how the horses got out?"

"Nope. As soon as I saw them standing in the middle of the road—" Wes motioned to his truck "—I stopped and called you."

"You should contact the sheriff, Kat," Brody said.

"And tell him what? We don't have any proof that Clyde and Roger did this." Kat's shoulders drooped, and Brody resisted the urge to reassure her that everything would be okay, because he doubted it would. Clyde and Roger had to be stopped soon before one of their pranks went too far.

"Might be a break in the fence line," Wes said. "I'll ride the perimeter of the ranch tomorrow."

Kat nodded. "Let me know if you find anything suspicious."

"Sure thing." Wes tipped his hat, then got into his truck and drove onto the trail that led to the far side of the property and the line shack.

"He's drunk," Brody said.

"Wes is always plastered by the end of the day."

"You need to report this to the sheriff, Kat. You can't rely on Wes to cover your back."

"I don't have to rely on Wes—I have you."

If Kat had dumped a bucket of ice water on his head, Brody couldn't have been more stunned. What had he done or said to give Kat the impression she could count on him for the long haul?

"Let's not worry about it tonight. Tomorrow Wes will find where the horses escaped and repair that section of fence. Problem solved."

Neither spoke during the drive back to the foreman's cabin. Kat pulled into the ranch yard then escorted the injured gelding into the barn to clean the cut on its leg. Brody released the other horse into the paddock between the barns.

"Hey, Brody." Ricky jogged across the ranch yard. "Everything okay?"

"Yep. We rescued both horses."

"Were they hurt?"

"One has a scrape on his leg. Your mom's in the barn taking care of him."

"How'd they get free?"

"We're not sure. Wes is going to look for breaks in the fencing tomorrow. In the meantime, if you see anything suspicious tell your mom."

"Yeah, sure, but mostly I just hang out in the barns."

"What about when you sneak off to meet Stevie?"

Ricky's mouth dropped open. "How do you know about that?"

"Wasn't that long ago that I was a teenage boy with a crush on a girl."

"Are you gonna tell my mom?"

"Depends."

Ricky cast an anxious glance toward the barn. "On what?"

"On what you're doing with Stevie when you two are alone." Teasing the kid was kind of fun.

"I haven't forgotten our talk," Ricky said.

Brody cleared his throat. "Just remember, Stevie's your first crush. Chances are you two will date other people before you find that special person to settle down with. Even so, you'll always remember your first love, so treat her with respect."

"Do you remember your first love?" Ricky asked.

"Sure do. Marybeth Richards. She had long, red hair, a ton of freckles and could outspit every boy in fifth grade. It was love at first sight."

Ricky laughed. "Why'd you break up?"

"Marybeth left me for Todd Arnold. Todd could get four bounces when he skimmed a rock across the water. My record was two."

"Can I ask you a personal question?"

"Sure."

"How do you know if it's true love?"

"If you end up going to school in town next year, you'll be surrounded by lots of girls. If any of those girls make you feel the same things Stevie does, then you'll know what you felt for Stevie was just your hormones going crazy and not true love."

"Does the same go for girls?"

"'Fraid so." Brody shook his head. "Sorry, kid, but adolescence sucks."

"If you break up with a girl can you still be friends with her?"

"That depends." At the teen's frown, Brody clarified.

"Sex messes up relationships. It's easier to remain friends with a girl if you haven't slept with her."

"How come all this boy-girl stuff is so complicated?"

"It's been that way for centuries, Ricky, and I doubt it will ever change."

"I like Stevie because she's good at fishing. And she doesn't get all grossed out when she touches the bait."

"She sounds like the perfect kind of girl to be a guy's friend."

"Yeah, maybe you're right. We should stay friends. If we break up, I won't have anyone to fish with."

"Sounds like a plan." Brody checked the time. "It's getting late."

"I better finish my math homework. Pretty soon I have to take a placement test for school next fall."

"Good luck with that."

Ricky took two steps then stopped and faced Brody. "Do you have a girlfriend?"

Kat's face popped into Brody's mind. If he ever wanted a girlfriend, she would be the one he'd pick. "Nope."

"Do you think my mom would make a good girlfriend, because she does a lot of the same stuff guys do?"

Caught off guard by the question, Brody took his time answering. "Your mother's a nice woman and she works hard. She'll make some lucky guy a great girlfriend." More than a girlfriend. Kat would make the perfect life partner. "Why do you ask?"

"I guess my mom and dad aren't ever going to be

together." Ricky's gaze skipped over Brody. "I thought maybe you and her…"

"I'm not the right man for your mother, Ricky." Brody flashed a smile, hoping to lighten the mood. "Your mom's a special woman. One day the right man will come along."

"Yeah, okay. 'Night, Brody."

"'Night, Ricky."

Brody stood in the dark, wishing with all his heart he could be the right man for Kat. It didn't take much imagination on his part to picture him, Kat and Ricky living together as a family. The more time he spent with Kat and Ricky the more he yearned for a foothold in their lives, but Ricky and Kat deserved better than a cowboy who was broken on the inside.

MIDNIGHT.

Kat paced the length of the kitchen. She hadn't spoken to Brody since they'd retrieved the horses from the side of the road. By the time she'd finished tending the gelding's injury, Brody had retired to the trailer. She'd returned to the cabin and too wound up by the day's events to sleep, she'd washed and dried a load of laundry, balanced her checkbook, then had taken a shower and slipped into her nightgown. Bedtime came and went, Brody still on her mind.

Tonight she'd realized how much she'd come to rely on Brody—not just for his help mucking stalls but his moral support, too. She knew he was attracted to her—she'd felt his eyes follow her when they'd worked side by side in the horse barn. It had been longer than she cared to admit since she'd been intimate with a man. Day after day she focused on being a good mother, working hard to provide for her and Ricky. Then one look from Brody and all of a sudden she craved tender caresses, whispered words and steal-your-breath kisses.

What would it be like to forget her troubles, the future, the past—living only in the moment with Brody?

Before she second-guessed herself, she slipped on a jacket, slid her feet into her flip-flops then left the cabin, closing the door quietly behind her. When she reached the trailer, she discovered Brody sitting at the top of the steps.

"Can't sleep?" His husky whisper sent shivers down Kat's spine.

"No. You either?"

He patted the space next to him. There wasn't much room, but she managed to wiggle her hips between Brody and the handrail. Their bodies touched from shoulder to calf and she soaked up his warmth.

Neither said a word for the longest time. They both knew what was happening between them. They'd danced around their attraction to each other since the day they'd met. She slipped her arm through his and leaned her head against his shoulder, then closed her eyes.

Brody's hand moved to her knee. His fingers rubbed her cotton nightgown against her skin. "I don't want to hurt you, Kat."

"You won't." Brody couldn't hurt her. As much as she wished things were different between them, Kat understood that when the Bakers returned from Europe, Brody would hit the road. From now on Kat would cherish every minute left with him.

Brody trailed his finger down her neck, then beneath

the collar of her jacket. Kat wasn't aware of who moved first, but suddenly her breasts were crushed against Brody's chest and their mouths were locked in a heated embrace. When they came up for air, he whispered, "Tell me to stop."

"No."

He kissed her again, then stood and held out his hand. They went inside and Brody walked her backward through the trailer to the bedroom, where she collapsed on the mattress.

"I want you, Kat."

She curled a finger in invitation and Brody settled on the mattress next to her. Their caresses started out soft and tentative then grew bolder and surer. Clothes were discarded, strewn about the bedroom. Brody worshipped Kat's body with his hands and mouth until she feared she'd faint. Time passed in a blur of sensation then the room spun and Kat felt herself splinter into a million pieces. When she floated back to earth Brody lay next to her nuzzling her neck.

"That was incredible," she whispered.

He responded to her praise with more kisses, leaving a trail of heat across her breasts and belly. This time was for Brody. Kat slid her leg between his thighs and shoved, rolling him onto his back. Mindful of his healing toes, she acquainted herself with his body, searching for places that were ticklish or sensitive—giving those areas special attention. It wasn't long before Brody had reached his limit. He tugged his wallet from his jeans pocket and removed a condom, then sheathed himself.

"Are you sure, Kat?"

She clasped his face between her hands and pulled

his mouth closer. "Very sure." This time when the end came, Kat wasn't alone. And for once that was okay with her.

"You're the best thing that's happened to me and Ricky in a long time." She snuggled against Brody's side.

"You wouldn't say that if you knew the truth about me."

"There's nothing you can tell me that will change my mind about you." She kissed his shoulder. "You're a good man, Brody Murphy."

They cuddled for the longest time. No words were spoken—they did all their talking with kisses and caresses. Then out of the blue Brody spoke. "Kat."

"What?"

"I had a daughter."

Had? The breath in her lungs froze.

"Angel had been coughing for a week when my wife, Kelly, asked if she could take her to the medical clinic in town. We couldn't afford health insurance on my salary, so I told Kelly to hold off a while longer to see if Angel got better. I thought she'd just come down with a bad cold."

Brody sprang from the bed, startling Kat. He paced across the room, then faced her. "My daughter died because of my selfishness. Every day was about me." He stabbed himself in the chest with his finger. "About what I wanted in life. My goals. My desires."

Kat sat up in bed and tugged the sheet against her breasts. "I don't understand."

"Kelly wanted me to quit my job as a ranch hand and hire on at the meat processing plant in town. The job came with medical benefits. Kelly was smart like that—she considered the future and what was best for our family. I only thought about myself and what was best for me." Brody bowed his head.

"If I'd allowed Kelly to take Angel to the doctor right away our daughter would be alive today."

Kat's eyes burned with empathy.

"Angel grew worse and Kelly finally got it through my thick skull that our daughter was in real danger." Brody met Kat's gaze, his eyes shimmering with unshed tears. "I'll never forget Kelly's expression when the doctor told her they hadn't been able to save Angel."

Brody covered his face with his hands. "My daughter died because I wanted to be a cowboy instead of a meat packer."

A tear dribbled off Kat's chin and plopped onto the back of her hand. She searched for words to comfort Brody, but there were none. "I don't know what to say."

"There's nothing to say, because no matter how you twist the story it comes out the same—I caused Angel's death."

Kat finally understood why Brody had insisted she notify the sheriff about the hay fire. He'd seen her actions as selfish. As caring more about proving she could handle the job at the Wild Rose than keeping her son and the ranch safe. Kat's stomach churned with shame.

She'd worked hard to make something of herself but in her quest to prove she was qualified for the foreman position at the Wild Rose, she'd lost sight of what really mattered—Ricky.

"I can't imagine the pain you feel, Brody. And to be

honest, I can't even sit here and tell you that it wasn't your fault. Or that you shouldn't blame yourself." She'd condemn herself, too, if she was in his shoes. Kat left the bed, dragging the sheet with her. "What I can tell you is that even though you may have made bad choices, you aren't a bad person. You loved your daughter with all your heart. Angel knows you're sorry. She knows you love her. And she forgives you."

"I've heard all that bullshit before. Repent, forgive and move on. What about Kelly? Kelly has to live the rest of her life with guilt, too, because she didn't defy me and take Angel to the doctors when she'd wanted to."

Kat ached for Brody, but at the same time she felt blessed that she'd never experienced the pain of losing a child. At seventeen she hadn't been ready for motherhood, but she couldn't imagine her life without Ricky. "Everyone makes mistakes. If we could travel back in time we'd make amends to those we've hurt. But life doesn't work that way. We learn from the past and move forward."

Brody pressed her palm against his chest—his heart thundered beneath her fingertips. "Don't you see, Kat? I can't allow myself to care about anyone ever again."

"You can't keep punishing yourself."

"You make me feel things I don't deserve to feel," Brody said.

Her spirits soared at his confession.

"I'm no good for you and Ricky."

"Let us be the judge of that." Kat lifted her mouth to Brody's. If he let her, she'd heal his pain and soothe his wounded soul.

BRODY LAY IN THE DARKNESS, Kat snuggled against his side. She slept soundly and for that he was grateful.

A tear escaped his eye. He brushed it aside and clenched his jaw until pain shot through the bone. *Why?* Why had the Fates conspired against him by bringing Kat and Ricky into his life?

Had he been so desperate to make amends for Angel's death that he'd mistakenly believed helping a teenager and his mother would absolve him of his sins? Kat was the devil in disguise—taunting him, tempting him to forgive himself and reach for happiness.

Kat slid her leg between his thighs and pressed herself against him. He never imagined he'd feel this connected to another human being again. Her caresses melted the icy coating that had formed on his heart the night Angel died. He had to leave before Kat succeeded in convincing him to turn his back on the past.

Kat was too vibrant a woman to attach herself to a battered veteran like Brody. He couldn't say for certain when or if he'd stop waging war against himself. Kat was generous and kind with a heart of gold—a woman who deserved a strong man by her side. Brody wasn't strong—he was weak and full of holes that refused to scar over.

He savored the weight of Kat's body on his and nuzzled her hair. Breathed deeply of her almond-scented shampoo. He trailed his fingertips along her arm and burrowed his face in her neck, then rubbed his nose against her soft skin. Last but not least he rested his palm against her heart.

The clock on the nightstand read 2:30 a.m. He should

leave. Before Kat woke. Before the awkwardness set in. Before she convinced him to stay.

He'd told himself that he could remain at the Wild Rose as long as he kept his hands to himself. Tonight he'd crossed the line and had broken that promise.

Easing a leg off the side of the bed, he dug the toes of his uninjured foot in the carpet for balance, then he pulled his arm free from beneath Kat's shoulders. She moaned in her sleep and flipped onto her side. He stared at her silhouette, envying her strength. Fortitude. Resolve.

After he gathered his clothes from the floor, he escaped to the bathroom and dressed in the dark. *What about Ricky?* Brody should stay until the morning to say goodbye to the kid.

No goodbyes.

He left the bathroom and stopped at the foot of the bed. Even though God quit listening to him, he sent up a silent prayer, asking Him to keep Kat and Ricky safe. Then he packed his few belongings, scribbled a message to Kat and left the trailer.

As long as he put one foot in front of the other and moved forward, to nothing and to no one, Brody would survive.

Chapter Ten

"Things are going great, Mark." Kat crossed her fingers behind her back as she spoke on the phone to her boss. She stood on the front porch of the cabin staring at the empty spot in the driveway where Brody had parked his truck. Two weeks had passed since she and Brody had made love.

Fourteen long, lonely days.

"The weather's warming up. I heard on the news that temps might be above average for most of May."

Kat had trouble concentrating on the conversation because her mind wandered to Brody. She'd known all along that there could be no forever with the bull rider, but she deserved better from him than his sneaking out in the middle of the night without so much as a goodbye. They'd made love—connected on an emotional level, which made his actions sting even more. The note he'd left tacked to the trailer door had left a hollow ache in her chest.

I'm sorry, Kat. B.

Not even a *please say goodbye to Ricky for me.* Brody might be gone physically but he still tormented her sleep. Each night when Kat fell into bed, visions of Brody and a faceless little girl disturbed her sleep.

Brody pushing his daughter on a park swing, then the child vanished, leaving him standing alone clutching a rag doll.

Brody standing at his daughter's hospital bedside, the little girl's skin cold and blue.

Brody walking through the mist calling Angel's name.

The love in Brody's eyes when he'd spoken of Angel haunted Kat. She was a healer and her first instinct was to ease his pain. But the grief of losing a child lasted a lifetime.

She couldn't imagine how she'd live without Ricky. Her son was her whole world. Everything she did was because of him. For him. She looked forward to watching him mature into a decent, productive, honest young man. All her hopes and dreams lived in Ricky. How Brody had found the strength to go on after Angel had died was beyond her understanding.

As much as she wanted to be the one to heal Brody's broken heart, the risk to her and Ricky was too great. If Kat ever found the courage to take a chance on loving again, she wanted to be the center of that man's universe. Because of what had happened to Angel, Brody would never allow himself to love another human being with all his heart and soul. She didn't want to have to fight for a man's love only to be rejected in the end.

She'd grown up never knowing her father, and looking back on her relationship with Dwayne, Kat supposed she'd expected him to fill the void in her heart. Dwayne had only cared about himself. Years later, after she'd matured and had met Seth, she'd been positive he'd felt the same love for her that she'd felt for him. She'd been disappointed again. Seth had decided he wasn't cut out for fatherhood after being in a relationship with her for almost a year. Ricky had been nine at the time and devastated when Seth had left. As much as it pained her to do so, Kat would mind her own business and leave Brody to wrestle his demons by himself.

Mark changed subjects and asked about the hay crop. "We brought the hay in before the rain and Tiger's hoof is beginning to heal now." Kat considered confessing that Clyde and Roger had walked off the job, but feared the Bakers would cut their vacation short and return to the ranch. Wes had yet to find any breaks in the fence line, which meant the perpetrator had opened the pasture gate and set the horses free to wander onto the road.

Mark mentioned touring the Eiffel Tower and Kat listened with half an ear. Five minutes later he ended the conversation. The instant she snapped her cell phone shut, Ricky opened the cabin door and rubbed sleep from his eyes. "How come you didn't wake me up this morning?"

"I thought you could use the extra rest." She ruffled his hair. Ricky had put on a brave face when he'd learned Brody had departed, but Kat sensed her son was deeply hurt that Brody hadn't cared enough to say goodbye in person.

"Hungry?" Most mornings Ricky fended for himself because she was out with the horses, but today Kat was the needy one and wanted her son by her side. "Are you in the mood for pancakes?"

"Sure." Ricky followed her into the kitchen, then

pulled out a chair and sat at the table. "Did Brody call?"

The same question every morning. "No, honey, he didn't."

"You think he'll come back?"

She swallowed a sigh. "No. Brody was eager to get back to riding bulls."

"I thought he was gonna stay at the Wild Rose until the Bakers came home."

Me, too, honey. "Guess he had a change of heart." Kat poured the batter on the grill, then set the table and warmed the syrup. "What's the matter?" she asked, alarmed by her son's despondent attitude.

"I'm tired of chores."

After Brody left, Ricky had to take over mucking stalls. By the time he finished cleaning the barn and doing his schoolwork, there wasn't much daylight left to fish with Stevie—probably a good thing considering the teens were obsessed with each other.

"When the Bakers return in a couple of weeks, they'll hire more cowboys and you won't have to help out as much." Ricky might not have to do any work if the Bakers fired Kat once they discovered what had transpired under her watch.

"Go after Brody, Mom. Ask him to come back. Tell him we really need his help."

"I wouldn't have any idea where to look for him. Besides, I can't leave the ranch." Her responsibility to the Bakers trumped her feelings for Brody. The ranch—not the cowboy—offered her and Ricky their best chance for stability and happiness.

"I bet I could find him," Ricky said.

"Don't even think about searching for Brody, young man." The last thing she needed was her son skipping off to who-knew-where without telling her.

"I don't get it. If Brody—"

"As soon as you're finished with breakfast, do your homework, then come out to the barn." She made it to the door before Ricky's question stopped her.

"What if the Bakers offered Brody a permanent job at the ranch? Would he stay then?"

"Leave it be, Ricky." *Brody made his choice.*

Now Kat was making hers. "You and I are just fine on our own."

TWO HOURS HAD PASSED and Ricky had yet to meet Kat in the barn. Frustrated, she grabbed the pitchfork and began mucking a stall. She was determined to keep the Wild Rose in good shape with or without anyone's help.

"Heard your bull rider moved on."

The deep voice slapped Kat in the back of the head and she froze for a split second. Clutching the pitchfork with both hands, she slowly turned. Roger and Clyde stood at the other end of the barn. "What do you want?"

"Our jobs back." Roger punctuated his statement by spitting tobacco on the clean floor.

"I don't need your kind of help."

Clyde snickered. "Maybe if we'd been workin' here them two horses wouldn't have ended up on the road a while back."

Just as Brody had guessed, the bastards had been

responsible for freeing the geldings. Kat played dumb. "What horses are you talking about?"

Her question caught the men off guard and they exchanged frowns. Then Clyde blurted, "The horses we let loose."

Roger shoved his elbow in his sidekick's ribs.

"Ouch! Quit it, would ya?" Clyde rubbed his side.

"I guess you two wouldn't happen to know anything about the fire in the hay field?" Kat asked.

Roger inched forward, stopping when Kat pointed the prong end of the pitchfork at him. "You got any proof we set that fire?"

"Not unless your fingerprints are on the gas can you left at the edge of the field." Roger's face paled. "Get off the ranch or I'll call the sheriff."

"I'm scared," Clyde said. "How 'bout you, Roger? You scared?"

"Shakin' in my boots." Roger cleared his throat. "I'll make you a deal, missy. We come back to work for the Wild Rose and we won't say nothin' to the Bakers about you messin' with that bull rider while you was supposed to be runnin' the place."

Kat scoffed. "The Bakers know I hired Brody because you two walked off the job." Kat hoped the lie would send the men searching for work far from Bandera.

"Why you—" Roger took a menacing step forward, but Kat jabbed the pitchfork at him. "I'm not afraid to use this."

"You'd better watch your back, missy. And that kid of yours, too. Wouldn't want either of you sufferin' an unfortunate accident."

A sound near the front of the barn caught Kat's

attention and she looked up in time to see Ricky skid to a halt inside the doors. Eyes wide he stared at the cowboys. "What's going on, Mom?"

Kat backed up a step. "Don't worry. These gentlemen were just leaving." Indecision warred in Roger's eyes then he cursed. "Be seein' you 'round, missy."

The men left the barn and Kat followed, breathing a sigh of relief when they drove off without making a scene.

"Were they gonna hurt you, Mom?"

"Don't worry, honey. Guys like Clyde and Roger are all bark and no bite." Kat changed the subject. "Did you finish your homework?"

"No."

Great. "C'mon, Ricky. Do your homework, okay? I need you to help muck stalls today."

Ricky grumbled beneath his breath as he trudged back to the cabin. Kat called after him. "I'll be up in an hour to make us some lunch."

As soon as the cabin door shut behind Ricky Kat pulled her cell phone from her pocket. Wes answered on the first ring. "Clyde and Roger were just here. They threatened to harm Ricky and me if I didn't hire them back." Her eyes strayed to the trailer, wishing Brody was inside.

"Call the sheriff. Melissa would want you to notify the authorities."

So would Brody.

Remembering Brody's accusation that her actions reflected her own agenda and not what was best for Ricky or the ranch, Kat conceded defeat. "I'll phone the sheriff right now, but keep your eyes peeled for any trouble."

By the time Kat ended her chat with the sheriff, she'd answered a slew of questions, including several about Brody. Because Clyde and Roger had worked for the Bakers almost five years, the sheriff preferred to believe Brody was the culprit and not the former ranch hands. When Kat explained that Clyde and Roger had refused to take orders from her, the sheriff sided with the cowboys, insisting any man with an ounce of pride would have walked off the job. The good-ol'-boy system was alive and well in Texas Hill Country.

Kat spent the next hour and a half tidying the horse stalls while her temper cooled. With the barn in order, she broke for lunch. Silence greeted her when she entered the cabin. "Ricky?" She hurried down the hall and flung open his bedroom door. Empty. She checked the bathroom. Empty. She returned to the main room where she saw the note on the kitchen counter.

I went to find Brody. He'll come back and help us.

Dear God. Ricky had run off again. She checked the clock. Her son had a two-hour head start. He'd probably hitched a ride by now—but to where?

Today Brody could be in a hundred different Texas towns hosting rodeos. Ignoring the panic building inside her, Kat grabbed the truck keys off the kitchen table and left the cabin. She whistled for Spot, not wanting to leave the dog behind for fear Clyde and Roger might return and harm him. As she sped down the ranch road, Kat phoned Wes and left a message on his cell that she was searching for Ricky.

Kat reached the main road and headed into Bandera, hoping she'd pass her son along the way. If not, she'd drive across the entire state of Texas if that's what it took to find him.

"HEY, BRODY! BRODY!"

Brody stopped and gaped. *What in the heck was Ricky doing in Boerne?* He scanned the crowd, searching for Kat, but she was nowhere in sight.

"I was looking for you," Ricky said, gasping for air.

A sharp twinge pierced Brody's side. Since he'd left the Wild Rose, not a day had gone by that he hadn't thought of the kid and his mother. "What are you doing here?" Brody recoiled at the harsh tone in his voice.

"You left without saying goodbye," Ricky accused.

Brody's stomach took a nosedive. He considered making up an excuse but the kid deserved better. "I don't like goodbyes." Ricky remained silent. "I'm guessing you ran off again without telling your mom."

"I didn't have a choice." Ricky's chin jutted. "Mom's in trouble and I knew you'd help if I could find you."

Apprehension squeezed Brody's lungs. He snagged Ricky's arm, pulling him aside, away from the crowd. "What kind of trouble?"

"Clyde and Roger threatened me and Mom."

"Threatened how?"

Ricky shrugged free of Brody's hold. "They said a bunch of mean stuff and told Mom if she didn't hire them back bad things might happen to us."

Brody's heart thumped painfully at the thought of Kat or Ricky coming to harm. "How did you know where to find me?"

"You left your rodeo schedule in the trailer."

So that's where he'd misplaced the calendar.

"You circled a bunch of places so I looked at today's date and saw that there was a rodeo in Boerne."

Smart kid. "We'd better call your mom, so she won't worry."

Brody skirted the stock pens and cut across the parking lot to where a handful of trucks and horse trailers sat parked. "Hey, Parker!" Brody called to the bronc rider who chatted with a group of buckle bunnies. Ed Parker excused himself from the ladies. "What's up?"

"Ed, this a friend of mine—" Brody scowled at Ricky "—who left home today without telling his mother. Mind if he borrows your cell, so he can check in with her?"

"Sure." Parker removed his phone from his pocket and handed it to Ricky. The teen walked a few feet away and dialed Kat's number.

"You see much of Drew Rawlins these days?" Parker said.

Brody shook his head. "Nope. He's busy getting his cutting horse ranch off the ground."

"Rawlins would have won the title if he hadn't scratched his ride at the finals. Shoot, every Vegas newspaper headline that week had his name in it."

"We'll never know." Brody doubted Rawlins even cared about the title. He was happy in his role as a father and husband.

Ricky returned and handed the phone to Parker. "Thanks," he muttered.

"What did your mom say?" Brody asked.

"She's on her way." Ricky shuffled his feet, then blurted, "I wanna stay and watch you ride."

"You'll get your wish, kid. I'm up in fifteen minutes."

"You can watch behind the chutes with me if you want," Parker said.

"Do you ride bulls like Brody?" Ricky asked.

Parker chuckled. "Hell no. I'm smarter than that. I bust broncs."

"You stick with Ed and don't wander off, you hear?" Brody said.

"Yeah, I hear."

As Ricky and Parker walked away, Brody silently cursed. He'd known in his gut that Clyde and Roger hadn't been finished with the Wild Rose.

Yet you still left.

He was a yellow-bellied coward. Guilt and worry had eaten away at Brody every minute of every day since he'd departed Bandera, but fear of the past catching up with him had kept him on the move.

Brody weaved through the crowd and made his way to the cowboy ready area, his mind on Kat and not Red Onion, the bull he'd drawn today. Brody didn't want to face Kat. He tossed his gear bag by chute number seven and removed his bull rope. The bell attached to the end of the rope clanked against his knee and Brody hissed at the sting it left behind.

"Well, big boy." Brody peered between the slats and eyed the bull. Red Onion turned his head and sprayed snot across the front of Brody's shirt.

"That all you got for me?" Brody dug out his riding

glove and put it on, then used his black rosin bag to make sure the leather was nice and tacky before he scaled the rails and straddled the bull. Most cowboys in this event wore protective headgear along with vests. Brody didn't bother with a helmet. He figured a kick in the head might knock some sense into him.

"Ready when you are," the cowboy on the other side of the cage said.

Brody lowered the rope down the side of the bull and his helper slid the end under the bull's chest then handed it back to Brody who pulled the rope over the withers, making sure the sewn-in handle was centered behind the animal's shoulders. Satisfied with the rope's placement, Brody slid the free end through the knot and pulled the rope tight. Red Onion rebelled, stomping and snorting.

A minute passed before the bull relaxed and Brody settled onto the animal's back. Once more he wrapped the free end tightly around his hand, securing it to the bull rope.

"Ladies and gentlemen, it's time for the world's first extreme sport…bull ridin'!"

The meager crowd clapped and a few rowdy fans stomped their feet. Brody glanced behind the chutes and spotted Ricky. He gave the thumbs-up sign and Ricky returned the gesture.

At least Kat isn't here to see you fall flat on your face or ass—whichever end hit the dirt first.

"Think you're scary, huh, big fella?" Red Onion kicked his back legs against the cage. The bull was a chute fighter and Brody prayed the announcer would finish his spiel before Red Onion became too restless and Brody had to hop off.

"Ladies and gents, today's first place winner in the bull ridin' competition takes home a thousand dollars."

A thousand dollars would keep Brody on the move for a long while and he wouldn't have to worry about finding part-time work to pay his entry fees.

"Turn your attention to chute number seven! Brody Murphy from Montana is gonna try to tame Red Onion, a first-rate bucker from the Kingsley Ranch outside Oklahoma City."

The dang bull garnered more applause than Brody.

Brody turned his thoughts inward, but instead of picturing his ride, Kat's face materialized before his eyes.

"Murphy's been bustin' bulls for a couple of years now and is still looking for his first win. Let's give Murphy some extra encouragement today." If not for Ricky watching, Brody couldn't have cared less about winning. For the kid's sake he'd try to make it to eight.

The announcer ran down a list of rodeo sponsors and Brody lost his concentration. Forcing himself to focus, he shut his eyes. No good. A slide show of Kat's face, displaying a thousand different emotions, fast-forwarded through his brain. He shook his head, hoping to dispel the images. The gateman misinterpreted Brody's gesture and the chute door suddenly opened.

Red Onion bolted for freedom. The first buck wasn't bad. Brody managed to stay seated and maintain a forward position, preventing himself from being tossed over the bull's head.

Red Onion bucked harder the second time and spun his two-thousand-pound girth to the right, flinging Brody about like a rag doll. He clenched his thighs against the bull's sides until fire licked his muscles.

The stands blurred before Brody's eyes as Red Onion went into a series of spins. Nausea worked its way up Brody's throat. He prayed for the buzzer but feared only a few seconds had passed since the chute door had opened.

C'mon. Stay on this time. Win this go-round for Ricky.

Red Onion came out of the spin and straight into a twisting buck. Brody slipped sideways. Clenching his teeth, he fought to keep his seat. Just when he'd gained control of his body, the stupid beast went into a belly roll—all four legs came off the ground and the bull kicked them in a twisting, rolling motion that sent Brody sailing through the air just as the buzzer sounded.

His right shoulder slammed into the ground first, knocking the air from his lungs. He rolled away from the bull, but as he attempted to stand he forgot about his broken toes and pushed off too hard on his injured foot. His leg buckled and he fell to the ground. The bullfighters closed in on Red Onion but the stubborn beast continued to spin and buck wildly.

The ground vibrated beneath Brody and dust swirled in the air. Eyes watering from the dirt the bull kicked in his face, Brody managed to get to his hands and knees. Red Onion charged. The bullfighters gave chase, but Red Onion kept coming.

Brody's last thought as he stared into the bull's eyes was Ricky. He didn't want the kid to see him go down this way. With a final burst of energy, Brody planted his feet on the ground and launched himself sideways. The bull ran past him, but not before Brody felt one of the animal's hooves kick the back of his calf. He'd have a nice bruise in the morning.

The bullfighters corralled Red Onion at the far end of the arena, while Brody stumbled to his feet. His toes hurt like hell and his calf muscle throbbed, but he limped through the pain and managed to bend down and sweep his hat off the ground. At least Red Onion had spared his favorite hat. He nodded to the crowd then exited through the gate.

"Well, folks. Too dang bad Murphy couldn't have held his seat for one more second. That was a hell of a ride."

"You were awesome, Brody!" Ricky's excitement faded and he frowned. "Are you okay? I thought Red Onion was gonna trample you after he bucked you off."

"I'm right as rain, Ricky." He nodded to Parker. "Thanks for letting Ricky hang out with you during my ride."

Parker patted Ricky on the back and walked away. "Nice to meet you, kid."

"Hungry?" Brody limped off, Ricky skipping alongside him.

"I'm always hungry."

"Let's grab a chili dog." Brody confiscated his bull rope and stuffed it into the gear bag then led the way to the concession stand.

They ordered their food and sat at a table near the parking lot. Ricky wasn't too talkative, which suited Brody just fine. His body ached all over and he wasn't in the mood for conversation. They'd sat at the table for almost an hour when a silver Ford with the Wild Rose logo on the door pulled into the parking lot. "Your mom's here. Looks like Spot came along for the ride, too." The dog's head stuck out the passenger-side window, his tongue flapping.

"How long do you think she's gonna ground me for?" Ricky asked.

"The rest of your life." Brody swallowed a chuckle at the teen's dejected face.

Chapter Eleven

Brody watched Kat search for a parking spot at the Boerne fairgrounds. She ended up in the last row. She left the truck and walked toward the main gate. Spot remained in the front seat. Brody waved his arm in the air and caught Kat's attention. She veered from the entrance and cut across the lot, her short strides eating up the gravel and sending plumes of dust into the air.

The knot in Brody's stomach cinched tighter. She looked good. Too good. He studied her face and his thoughts turned to the night they'd made love. His skin burned with the memory of her caresses—her leg sliding between his. Her fingers blazing a path across his stomach. Her back arching off the bed when he—God, he missed her.

Missed her subtle smiles. The scent of her shampoo. The soft look in her eyes when she stared at her son. He even missed her take-charge attitude and stubborn pride. He was fooling himself if he believed he'd escaped the Wild Rose before Kat had left her mark on him.

Kat was the perfect woman to help him put his life back on track, but Brody knew in his gut he couldn't live up to her high expectations and he refused to join the group of men who'd already disappointed her.

"She looks mad," Ricky said.

Kat's pinched expression didn't bode well for the kid. Or Brody.

"Stevie wanted me to go fishing with her and her dad next weekend. Guess that's out."

Brody fought a grin. "The only fishing you'll most likely do in the near future will be scooping moss from the horse troughs."

"I was trying to help."

"I know, son, but——" Brody held his breath. The word *son* had just slipped out. *Get a grip before you do something stupid like pretend Kat and Ricky are yours to worry about.* "Remember something while your mom's yelling at you—she loves you and you're the most important person in her life. If anything happened to you she'd never forgive herself." *Believe me, kid, I know all about not being able to forgive yourself.*

Ricky unfolded his long legs and met his mother halfway. They stared at one another for a second, then Kat opened her arms and Ricky stepped into her hug.

Brody's throat tightened at the sight of the pair. The hug lasted a good long while then Kat's pointer finger went into action. Brody heard bits and pieces of the scolding Ricky received, and Kat's voice broke twice during the reprimand—behind her anger was an intense relief that no harm had befallen her son.

Kat's tirade ended abruptly. She hugged Ricky one more time then the teen saluted Brody before returning to the truck. Kat remained where she was and a stare-down ensued.

Brody waited, not sure what she expected from him. When he'd left the ranch he'd never intended to see Kat again. Giving in first, she broke eye contact and continued in his direction. She stopped a few feet from the table.

"Brody."

"Kat."

She perched her hands on her hips as if ready to do battle, but the longing in her stare caught Brody by surprise. He held her gaze, not caring if his eyes mirrored her emotions. "Thank you for looking after Ricky until I could get here."

"I'm glad he found me." Brody gripped the edge of the table to keep from leaving his seat and sweeping Kat into his arms. He wanted to kiss her so damned bad.

"You didn't say goodbye." The lashes of her pretty brown eyes fluttered. He prayed she wasn't blinking back tears.

"Like I told Ricky, I hate goodbyes."

"I deserved a goodbye, Brody."

You deserved more than a goodbye. "I was afraid."

She toed a piece of gravel with her boot heel. "Afraid of what?"

Afraid of trying to be the kind of man you need and deserve. "I'm not good enough for you, Kat."

Her eyes widened. "Who said I was looking for a long-term relationship? I said you could leave anytime no hard feelings, but you led me to believe you were helping out until the Bakers returned."

Kat's words were more painful than his stinging calf muscle. Had he misjudged her feelings for him? She cared for him—maybe even a lot—but her words had made it clear she didn't love him.

"I'm a grown woman who's been on my own for a long time. I'm raising my son without the help of his father. And I've supported myself and Ricky most of my adult life. I don't need a man." She narrowed her eyes. "Especially one I can't trust."

Brody left his seat at the picnic table and closed the distance between them.

There was no way he could send Kat and Ricky back to the Wild Rose alone. He couldn't take the chance that Clyde or Roger would…If something happened to…There was no room left in his conscience for more guilt.

Now that he knew where he stood with Kat—she didn't need or want anything more from him than his help with ranch chores—he could survive another week or two in her company before moving on. Couldn't he? "I'll follow you and Ricky back to the ranch."

"I…" Kat stared into space, chin trembling. "Fine." She spun on her boot heels and marched to the truck.

Brody crossed the lot to his vehicle. For a while longer he'd pretend he was part of a family. The moment the Bakers returned, he'd leave the area—this time for good. And with no regrets.

LATE THURSDAY AFTERNOON, Brody watched Kat out of the corner of his eye. He was having a heck of a time avoiding her since he'd returned to the ranch six days ago. He'd kept conversation to a minimum, choosing to spend his free time with Ricky. He made sure he turned out the lights in the trailer promptly at ten each night then he'd lie in bed praying Kat would knock on the door. Praying she wouldn't.

He worked himself to the bone during the day but his nights remained sleepless. He wanted Kat—wanted the closeness he'd felt with her when they'd made love. He was a big boy who'd been knocked around by life in big ways, yet his need for Kat was more than physical—she soothed his soul.

Kat moved sideways, offering Brody a better view of her curvy backside. She prodded Tiger's hoof, muttering quietly beneath her breath. Brody hated that Kat had made it easy for him to keep to himself. In her quiet, determined way she gave him a list of chores each day then left him alone. As much as Brody believed it was best, he wished Kat would send him a signal that she was ready to forgive and forget, because he ached to put an end to this yearning inside him.

Kat glanced up and their gazes clashed. For an instant her eyes darkened—the same heated look she'd given him the night they'd made love. The sizzle died a quick death when her expression sobered. She wiped her sweating brow with the sleeve of her shirt.

"Where's Ricky?" The last time Brody had seen the kid he'd been throwing a stick to Spot in the ranch yard.

"He went fishing with Stevie," she said.

"What happened to being grounded the rest of the summer?"

"What can I say?" She laughed, but the sound lacked humor. "I suck at parenting."

"Nah, you have a soft heart is all." *And you take in strays like me.* "How'd he get to Stevie's?"

"He rode his dirt bike." She held up a hand. "I made him wear a helmet."

Brody and Kat were all alone. "Have you heard from Wes today?"

"Nope. No news is good news."

The afternoon following the Boerne rodeo, Brody had saddled up a horse and ridden the perimeter of the property, searching for signs that Clyde and Roger were up to their old tricks. He'd found nothing amiss. Two nights ago he'd driven out to Dicky's Roadhouse and had asked the bartender if the ranch hands had stopped in for a beer lately—the man couldn't remember.

"After I fill the feed bins I'll take a ride around the property."

"That would be great, thanks." Kat's stiff posture relaxed. "I've got a horse to shoe after I finish with Tiger."

Brody's gaze clung to Kat's. What could one kiss hurt if it didn't lead anywhere? *Move, Brody. Move.* He did—only in the wrong direction. He stepped forward, lowered his head and he saw Kat's lips part as if in invitation… The slamming of a truck door shocked Brody back to his senses and he stepped away from Kat.

Wes strolled into the barn. "We got trouble. The stream's dammed up in the north pasture and the waters flooding the—"

"Oh, no, not the hay," Kat said.

There were three separate pastures used to grow organic hay at the Wild Rose. Each section of land was planted on a rotational system so there was always freshly cut hay available for sale. The hay in the north pasture wouldn't be ready to harvest until the end of next month, which meant a flood at this stage of the growing process would result in the loss of the crop.

"What do you want me to do, Kat?" Brody said.

"Grab the handsaw and bring a set of chains. Wes, you round up the horses near the stream and put them in another pasture."

"Already did that," Wes said.

"Good. In case this wasn't our friend Mr. Beaver that caused the logjam, keep your eyes peeled for trouble elsewhere on the ranch."

"Will do."

Kat hurried through the barn. "We'll take your truck, Brody. It's got a bigger engine if we need to move large branches. I'm heading up to the cabin to leave Ricky a note."

BRODY DROVE IN SILENCE along a service road that cut through the horse pastures. The tension in the truck grated on his nerves and he strangled the steering wheel, wondering what had gotten into him a few moments ago. He never should have tried to kiss Kat, but he'd caved in to the temptation that had eaten at him the past week.

Maybe he should apologize.

You'll just make it worse.

Before Brody decided what to do, they arrived at the stream. He whistled low between his teeth. The hay field had turned into a pond. Flashing lights caught his attention in the rearview mirror. A patrol car stopped behind Brody's truck. "The sheriff's here."

"I called him." Kat hopped out of the front seat and Brody followed. "Sheriff Conrad, this is Brody Murphy.

He's the man I told you about who's been helping out at the ranch."

Brody shook the sheriff's hand. "Nice to meet you."

The sheriff studied Brody. "Heard you were from Montana."

"Yes, sir."

"What brought you down here to Texas?"

"Brody's a bull rider," Kat said.

"That explains it. We got rodeos every weekend in this great state."

"Those tree limbs—" Brody pointed to the pile of debris across the stream "—were strategically arranged to force the water over the banks and into the field."

"I can see that for myself, young man." Sheriff Conrad shielded his eyes from the sun. "Yep. That sure don't look like any beaver jam I've ever seen."

"Wait here." Brody waded into the water, stopping in the middle of the streambed. "I'll be damned."

"What do you see?" the sheriff asked.

"Five maybe six hay bales at the bottom of the stream." Beavers didn't sneak into storage barns and drag off sixty-pound hay bales. Brody waded toward the pile. "The branches are clean-cut." He studied the stand of trees across the pasture. The tree branches appeared undisturbed. The branches had been sawed off a tree elsewhere and hauled into the pasture.

"Clyde and Roger did this," Kat said, as Brody made his way back to dry land.

"You sure you want to accuse them of sabotaging their former employer's property?" Sheriff Conrad asked.

"Yes, I'm sure." Kat walked along the mushy stream bank, shaking her head.

"Did you tell Sheriff Conrad about the fire and the horses getting free?" If Kat wouldn't, Brody would.

"Kat told me Wes discovered a pile of smoldering hay after the field had been cut and she did mention the horses that got loose on the road," Sheriff Conrad said.

Brody was happy Kat had finally taken his advice and informed the authorities. "I'd bet my life that the same culprits are responsible for this mess."

"I'll need to take pictures before you clean this mess up." The sheriff returned to his patrol car and retrieved a camera, then snapped a few photos.

"You'll order your deputies to be on the lookout for Clyde and Roger, right?" Brody said when the sheriff put the camera away.

"Let's not jump to conclusions about those men. Ranch hands are known to play a few pranks when they've been wronged."

"They weren't wronged. Kat acted well within the bounds of her authority," Brody said. "I've worked as a ranch hand my entire adult life. You follow orders or you get fired. Clyde and Roger not only ignored Kat's authority they made personal threats against her and her son."

The sheriff faced Kat. "Is there more going on than what you reported the other week?"

"Clyde and Roger approached me in the barn and demanded their jobs back. I refused, so they threatened me and Ricky."

"What kind of threat?" the sheriff asked.

"They hinted that my son or I might suffer an unfortunate accident."

The sheriff scowled. "All right then. I'll have my deputies bring Clyde and Roger in for questioning if they run across the men. In the meantime be careful and report anything unusual as soon as it happens." The sheriff got into his patrol car and drove off.

"Where do we begin?" Kat asked.

"With the big limb on top of the pile. I'll grab the chains and the winch hook." Brody took one end of the chain and waded into the stream then wrapped it around the thickest part of the limb. He dragged the heavy chain back through the water and to his truck where he clamped the ends together with a winch hook, then secured the chain to the trailer hitch.

"Watch out." Brody stuck his foot inside the cab and pressed the gas pedal. The limb slid sideways, but didn't break free from the pile.

"Must be caught. See if you can wiggle it loose, Kat, then I'll try again."

Kat waded into the stream, then called over her shoulder, "The end of the limb is stuck in the mud."

"Can you move the chain lower?" Brody asked.

"I'll try."

While Kat did as he asked, Brody waited for her signal. She raised her arm and he pressed the gas pedal. The truck tires spun in the mud. He checked the rearview mirror. Kat moved farther into the creek, the water rising to her chest. She shoved her shoulder against the limb and he pressed on the gas. The truck lurched forward. Success!

He put the truck into Park and hopped out. "We

did—" Where was she? Panic swept through Brody as his eyes scanned the stream. Had Kat been knocked unconscious by the limb when it broke free? He ran into the creek, the sandy bottom sucking at his boot heels, slowing his progress. "Kaaat!"

Aeons passed before he reached the debris pile. He shoved, pushed and clawed at the branches, searching for Kat's red shirt. He swept his arm through the water and his fingers tangled with her hair. He dived under, grabbed Kat around her middle and tugged hard until her head cleared the surface.

"Foot's stuck!" she gasped, before her head disappeared beneath the water.

Brody dived under, skimming his hands down her leg to where her boot was buried deep in the muck. The massive branch they'd moved off the pile must have left a hole in the streambed and Kat's foot had been sucked into it. Lungs burning, he scooped sand away from her boot, but sediment immediately filled in the hole.

Needing air, he surfaced, bringing Kat with him.

"My foot's sinking deeper," Kat gasped, her head slipping below the water.

Brody lifted her body so her chin cleared the water's surface. "Your foot has to come out of the boot."

"I can't. There's mud inside."

Brody went under again and grasped Kat's calf. He twisted and pulled, knowing his fingers would leave bruises on her skin. Her foot gave a little and Brody yanked harder. Finally, her foot slid free of the boot. He set his hand against her fanny and shoved her to the surface, the action causing him to swallow water.

He surfaced, coughing and sputtering, but was more

concerned about Kat. She clung to a tree branch, gasping for air. Brody rubbed her back then rested his forehead on her shoulder. Thank God Kat was okay.

"How's your foot?" he asked.

"It's numb." She leaned into him. "I could have..." Tears welled in her eyes.

"Shh..." He hugged her tight. "You're okay. C'mon. Let's get out of the water."

Kat leaned heavily against Brody as he guided her to dry land. When they reached the bank, they both collapsed.

Brody lay on his back staring at the sky, his heart thundering, his hands shaking. He'd almost lost Kat. For an instant when she'd disappeared from sight, Angel's face had popped into his mind and an all-consuming panic had taken his body prisoner.

Not again. Not again.

The thought of losing another person he loved had spurred him forward.

Dear God. Had he just admitted that he loved Kat? He rolled his head to the side and stared at her profile. Chest heaving, eyes closed, wet hair plastered to her face, Kat was...beautiful and *alive.* His throat tightened and he struggled to draw in a steadying breath. He couldn't do this again. He couldn't love another person more than life only to lose them because he hadn't protected them. He should have never asked Kat to stay in the stream and loosen the branch while he drove the truck. Kat was lucky the water hadn't been deeper, or the limb hadn't fallen and crushed her foot, the pain rendering her unconscious.

Because of him Kat could have drowned.

Because of him Ricky might have lost his mother.

The ache was sharp and biting and he cursed himself. Way back in March he should have driven straight to Drew's ranch as he'd planned and not stopped in Bandera. Not gone to the festival. Not teamed up with Ricky in the hog-catching contest. He choked on the knot in his throat. Thinking about never having met Kat was almost as painful as having to let her go.

No matter that Kat was the first woman since Angel's death who made him want to stop running, today was a wake-up call—he was no good for Kat.

"Are you okay?" she asked.

"Yeah." Brody got to his knees and shoved Kat's wet pant leg up. Carefully he peeled her sock off. "Your ankle's puffy." Marks from his fingers marred her calf. "Let's get you warm." He scooped Kat's shivering body into his arms and set her in the truck, then started the ignition and flipped on the heater.

"I'm going to adjust the chain around the large limb. I'll signal when I'm ready for you to hit the gas."

Removing the rest of the debris from the stream was exhausting and took Brody an hour. The sun was setting by the time he finished. "There's quite a bit of erosion where the stream flooded its bank. You'll want to shore up that area before the next rainstorm hits." Kat nodded but didn't speak. He guessed she was as worn-out as he was.

They arrived at the cabin and found Ricky sitting on the front porch with Spot. Catching sight of their disheveled appearance, the kid asked, "What happened to you guys?"

Kat managed a smile as she limped forward. "We had to clear a jam in the stream."

Ricky jogged to his mother's side, and helped her walk. "Did you get hurt?"

"Twisted my ankle. I'm afraid my boot's stuck in the bottom of the stream." At the porch steps, Kat said, "I'll start supper after I clean up."

"Don't worry about supper." Brody swept Kat into his arms and carried her up the steps and into the cabin. "I'll be back in a minute to make everyone a sandwich. You stay off your ankle."

Brody returned to the trailer where he showered and changed clothes. Twenty minutes later he was back in the cabin slapping bologna and mayo sandwiches together. Kat sat at the kitchen table with her leg propped on a chair and ice on her ankle. If not for Ricky's chatter about his fishing trip with Stevie the meal would have been a subdued affair.

Ricky helped Brody clean up the kitchen then the kid excused himself and retired to his room to watch TV. Brody went out to the barn where he spent the next three hours finishing Kat's chores. Afterward he hauled several bales of fresh hay into the horse barn so Kat would have plenty of feed on hand for a few weeks. When there was nothing more he could do, he returned to the trailer and settled in front of the TV, hoping the late-night news would take his mind off the day's events.

Chapter Twelve

Brody switched TV channels for the umpteenth time. Nothing grabbed his attention. Maybe he should call it a day. He turned off the TV and was halfway to the bedroom when he heard a knock. Reversing direction, he limped to the trailer door, mindful of his sore toes. Ricky stood on the steps. The kid didn't wait for an invitation. He stepped past Brody then sprawled across the love seat.

"Want something to drink?" Kat had been generous these past weeks and had kept the fridge stocked with a variety of beverages.

"No, thanks."

Brody returned to the recliner and propped his foot up. He waited for Ricky to speak, but the teen remained silent, his gaze stuck on the floor. "What's on your mind?"

"Stevie and I were talking about next fall." A determined look entered Ricky's eyes.

"And..."

"We really like each other, and we want to go to school together next year."

Although he sympathized with the teen, whether or

not Ricky attended school in Bandera wasn't any of his business.

"With all the trouble Mom's been having because of those jerks who quit, we might have to move. Mom said the Bakers probably won't let her to stay on, which means we'll have to go back to moving from place to place so she can find enough work." Ricky expelled a deep sigh. "And I'll have to be homeschooled again."

"Don't jump to conclusions. The Bakers sound like fair-minded people. They'll listen to your mom's side of the story before they make any decisions."

Ricky shrugged. "Stevie and I thought of an idea that would let Mom and me stay in the area even if the Bakers fire her."

Brody had a hunch he was going to regret asking. "What's your idea?"

"Mom likes you and you like my mom." Ricky's cheeks turned bright red. "Don't you?"

A flashing yellow light went off in Brody's head. He proceeded with caution. "I have a lot of respect for your mother, Ricky."

"Then maybe you could—" Ricky stared at his lap "—you know, marry her."

Where in the world had the kid come up with such a crazy idea? "I don't—"

"Wait. I want you to hear my plan before you say no." The teen popped off the couch and paced into the kitchen then back into the family room. "Remember when you said you suck at bull riding?"

Brody nodded.

"Maybe you could give up rodeo and just be a ranch

hand near here. Mom could go off during the day and shoe horses and I could go to school with Stevie."

Brody was speechless. Ricky on the other hand had plenty more to say. "I saw Mom sneaking out of the trailer a while back and it was late at night." Ricky peeked at Brody. "I figured, you know...that you two... you know..."

Great. Ricky knew his mother had slept with the hired hand. "I like your mother a lot, Ricky." *More than you'll ever know.* More than is safe. More than is sensible.

"Okay, so then it wouldn't be a big deal for you guys to get married. Right?"

"Wrong."

Ricky's face lost color and Brody cursed beneath his breath. He wasn't handling the situation well.

"You don't like me, do you?" Ricky blurted. Brody opened his mouth to deny the charge but the kid spoke over him. "I can change. I'll help out more with chores, and I won't play video games all the time. I'll quit sneaking off without telling Mom and—"

"Stop." Brody rubbed his hands down his face. "It's not you, Ricky."

"Then what is it?"

"Not what...who." Brody left the chair and went into the bedroom. He rummaged through his gear bag until he found what he was looking for. He walked back into the living room and handed Ricky the photograph.

"Who is she?"

"My daughter. Her name is...was Angel."

Ricky stared at the picture, his eyes wide. "What happened to her?"

"She died of pneumonia."

"How old was she?"

"Five."

"Do you have any more kids?"

"No." Brody swallowed hard. How did he explain to a thirteen-year-old that he was done being parent? "Ricky, I don't want to be responsible for raising a second child." Brody had no desire to ruin another kid's life.

"But you wouldn't have to worry about me. I'm Mom's responsibility, not yours."

If it were only that simple. Brody wanted to grant Ricky's wish, but didn't dare. "I'm sorry, kid. I'd like to help, but I can't."

Several minutes passed while Ricky studied Angel's image. "Do you think about her a lot?"

"Every minute of every day."

He set the photograph on the table. "Then she's lucky."

Lucky? Angel was dead. "How do you mean?"

"You miss her and you think about her. That's more than my dad cares about me." Ricky walked to the door. He hesitated, his hand on the knob.

Just go, kid.

"I'm sorry about your Angel, Brody." The door closed with a quiet click.

Brody snuffed out the lamp by the recliner and sat in the dark for a long time. Tears leaked from his eyes, but he didn't have the energy to wipe them away. He cried for Angel. He cried for Ricky. He cried for Kat. He cried until he fell asleep.

C'MON, BRODY, OPEN THE DOOR.

Kat tapped her foot impatiently. Ricky had been

unusually quiet after visiting Brody earlier in the evening. Her son had shocked her when he'd announced at ten o'clock that he was going to bed. Usually he remained awake past midnight, playing video games. Unable to sleep herself after the day's traumatic events, Kat had decided to take a piece of apple pie to Brody, since he'd skipped dessert.

She knocked again. No answer. He must have gone to bed. Just as she turned away, the door swung open. Her breath hitched. Brody's rumpled shirt was unsnapped, revealing a glimpse of his muscled chest. Without a belt, his jeans rode low on his hips, the elastic waistband of his white briefs visible. Dragging her eyes from his body she studied his face, noting his puffy eyes. "I woke you."

He ran his fingers through his sandy blond hair, leaving the strands standing on end. "I must have dozed off during the news." He stepped back from the door.

Kat slid past him, catching his scent—soap, deodorant and clean male. "Dessert." She shoved the plate at him.

"Thanks." He set the pie on the kitchen table.

Following a stilted silence, Kat sat on the bench seat and said, "I can't sleep."

Leaning against the counter, Brody crossed his arms. The wall clock ticked off seconds until he met her gaze, his blue eyes sending a jolt through Kat's body. "How's your ankle?" he asked.

"A little sore." She cleared her throat. "I called Mark Baker and explained what's happened since they left for Europe." Admitting defeat to her employer had been one of the most difficult tasks she'd faced in years, but she'd rather Mark hear the news from her than Sheriff Conrad. "I told Mark that I fired Clyde and Roger—" Kat's eyes burned, but she fought off tears "—because they refused to mow the hay or take orders from me." She blew out a gust of air. "Mark wasn't pleased."

"You did the right thing informing the Bakers."

"Mark said he and Melissa would cut their vacation short. They're returning on the sixteenth."

Brody remained quiet and for the first time since she'd entered the trailer, Kat felt a sense of unease. "Mark said he'd put a call in to the foreman at Indian Manor." The horse farm was twenty miles east of the Wild Rose. "Jim Mendel and Mark are good friends. He's going to ask Jim if he can spare one of his cowboys until Mark can interview and hire another ranch hand." Kat hadn't told the Bakers that she'd hired Brody to help out after Clyde and Roger left mainly because she hadn't wanted to answer a lot of personal questions about her relationship with Brody.

More silence.

"Ka—"

"Bro—"

Brody motioned for Kat to continue. "I wanted to tell you how grateful I am for all your help. I don't know what I would have done if you hadn't been here."

"You would have managed, Kat. You're a fighter."

Kat basked in his compliment. "Regardless, I couldn't have cleared the debris from the stream by myself. Ricky would have had to help and…" She shuddered as she pictured her son losing his footing in the streambed or becoming trapped beneath a tree limb.

"What are your plans if the Bakers don't offer you a permanent position?"

"I'll hitch the trailer to my truck and return to shoeing horses when and where I can find work." She hated the idea of uprooting her son again, but she'd do what was necessary to support them.

"What about Ricky wanting to go to school in Bandera?"

Kat picked at her nails and ignored the sharp pain in her chest. "He's a tough kid. He'll survive another disappointment if he has to." Kat yearned to make Ricky's wish to attend public school come true but the odds were stacked against her. She recalled a dream she'd had about the future... The Bakers had offered her a permanent job at the Wild Rose. Ricky made the football team at the junior high school. Brody competed in rodeos but lived with Kat and Ricky when he wasn't on the road. Reality was the polar opposite of her dream.

In a few years Ricky would strike out on his own and make a life for himself, leaving Kat behind. She wasn't afraid of being alone—she was afraid of being lonely. She wanted to share her life with a special man. She wished Brody could be that man.

Before she realized what she was saying, the words were out of her mouth. "Stay with us, Brody." His eyes widened with distress. Fearing rejection she rushed on. "Even after the Bakers return."

Brody's face turned ashen. "I can't."

Don't beg. Please don't beg. "Why?"

He didn't answer and a burning heat crept into her cheeks. Time to leave. Brody beat her to the door. His hot breath puffed against the top of her head. Gathering her courage she looked him in the eye. His tortured expression cut her to the quick.

"I don't want to leave, but…"

"Then don't," she whispered.

"It's not that simple."

Right then Kat decided she'd do anything to make Brody change his mind. She was certain that with time he'd reach the same conclusion she had—they were meant to be together.

But the stakes were high. She was halfway in love with Brody right now and it would take little effort on his part to win the other half of her heart. Giving no thought to the consequences, Kat snuggled her head beneath his chin. Heart thundering, she rubbed her nose against his clean skin and breathed in his scent. Then she kissed his neck, flicking her tongue over his hot skin. He moaned and cupped her breast, squeezing gently. She slid her thigh between his legs and nudged his groin, rejoicing in the hardness against her knee.

Confident they'd end up in bed, Kat poured her heart and soul into each caress and kiss, erasing any doubt in Brody's mind that she wanted him. She stood on tiptoe and lifted her face to his.

The woman drove him mad. Holding her head, he devoured her mouth. She tasted good. *So damned good.* Kissing Kat made Brody feel clean and innocent inside. She made him believe he could become a new man. A better man.

With a fierceness he hadn't known he'd possessed, Brody swung Kat into his arms and carried her to the bedroom. He laid her on the mattress, covering his body with hers. Time ceased as he lost himself in loving Kat.

Clothes were tossed on the floor and there was little need for foreplay. Kat was as eager for him as he was for her. Their lovemaking was fierce and wild—moans, groans and shuddering breaths.

Brody fought against the slow, steady throb building inside him…driving him crazy…making him desperate to prolong the experience. He attempted to shut off his emotions and focus on the physical sensations Kat's touches and kisses invoked. Brody yearned to take a leap of faith and pray that Kat would catch him…heal him…help him find peace. He wanted redemption so damned bad, but Kat had been hurt in the past. Brody couldn't promise that he wouldn't hurt her, too.

Angry and bitter that a future with Kat was out of his reach, he threw himself into his lovemaking, needing to show Kat how much he wished things could be different for them. The end came with such force that Brody felt gutted. As their bodies cooled, Kat's eyes fluttered open. "Don't leave, Brody."

First Ricky. Now Kat.

"I'm a bull rider, Kat. Rodeo cowboys don't put down roots." He buried his face between her breasts, his throat tight with need. Pain. Guilt. Her nails scraped against his skull as she slid her fingers through his hair. His body throbbed with renewed arousal.

Kat pushed his shoulders, forcing him to look her in the eye. "You're always welcome with Ricky and me wherever we are."

Another minute and he'd give in and accept what Kat offered—a future. Forgiveness. Maybe even love. The longer he remained at the Wild Rose the greater the risk of succumbing to a deeper need to be part of Kat's and Ricky's lives.

Brody sprang from the bed, grabbed his clothes and disappeared into the bathroom. A minute later he returned to the bedroom fully clothed. He stuffed his possessions into his duffel bag and without a word, he walked out of the room.

A sense of déjà vu filled Kat as she shielded her body with the sheet and trailed Brody to the door. "You can't run forever."

"I'm going to give it a hell of a try." Shoot, he'd missed too many rodeos as it was—not that he would have won any of them. No matter how hard he worked at the sport, bull riding wasn't in his blood. Brody sat in the recliner and tugged on his boots.

Kat's chest heaved with her struggle not to cry. Couldn't Brody see that what they had together was a hundred times better than what they had alone? That together they could face the future and conquer their fears?

"Angel wouldn't want you to live like this."

He faced Kat. "Live like what? In order to succeed at my job I need to compete in as many rodeos as possible."

"You're not a bull rider, Brody." Kat sighed, the sound coming from deep within her chest. "You're the worst competitor on the circuit." She knew for a fact because she'd researched the PRCA rodeo on the internet and his name never appeared in the winner's column.

"A man's luck can change."

"A man has to want his luck to change first," she said.

"What's that supposed to mean?"

"It means you believe you don't deserve any happiness in life because of what happened to your daughter." Desperate to find a way to keep Brody from leaving, she said, "You're tired of running and tired of paying for your daughter's death, but you don't have the guts to ask for forgiveness. When are you going to accept that you're human and humans make mistakes, especially with those they love most."

"That's enough, Kat."

She'd come this far.... "You ride bulls, because you're looking for an out. A way to make the pain stop. The guilt to go away."

"You think I'm on a suicide mission?" Brody's face transformed into an angry mask, his eyes cold and empty.

The tears she'd valiantly held at bay, escaped and she held out her hand, pleading in silence.

The quiet click of the door latch was a shotgun blast to her heart.

"HEY, MOM." Ricky sat at the kitchen table and shoved a half slice of buttered toast into his mouth.

Kat yawned for the hundredth time as she poured a glass of milk for her son. She'd lain awake for hours last night after Brody had departed. Finally she'd fallen asleep and the alarm on her cell phone had jarred her awake a half hour later.

She delivered the milk to Ricky then refilled her coffee cup, before joining him at the table.

"What's the matter? Are you sick?" Ricky frowned.

Heartsick. She blew on her coffee. "I didn't sleep well."

"You want me to feed the horses?"

Her son had rotten timing—deciding to be sweet when her defenses were weak. Tears burned her eyes and she sniffed.

"Jeez, Mom, don't cry. I'll help Brody muck stalls as long as I can go to Stevie's later this afternoon after she gets home from school. We're gonna watch *Scary Movie 3.*"

Friends. A social life. Kat had wanted those things for her son for so long. And now that he was finally happy—another disappointment loomed on the horizon. Life sure wasn't fair.

"I'll take you up on your offer to clean the barn." She forced the words past her lips. "Brody left."

Finished with his toast, Ricky dug into his scrambled eggs. "When's he coming back?"

"He's not. Brody decided to return to rodeoing."

"Like for a week or something?"

Heart aching, Kat shook her head. "For good."

Ricky shoved his plate aside and left the table. He opened the cabin door and stared at the gravel parking area as if sheer will would force Brody's truck to magically appear.

"Honey, I'm sorry he didn't get a chance to say goodbye, but he wanted me to tell—"

"Did he leave because of me?" Ricky slammed the door, his face white.

Kat popped out of her chair and hugged her son. That he didn't resist proved how Brody's absence upset him. "No, honey." *He left because of me.* Guilt flooded Kat. If only she hadn't gone to the trailer last night Brody might have stayed. "Why would you think Brody left because of you?"

"Because I asked him if he'd marry you, so we could stay in Bandera and I could go to school with Stevie next year."

Kat gasped.

"I saw you go to the trailer late one night and I thought you guys were…" Ricky's gaze skidded away.

Dear Lord. Ricky guessed she and Brody had… Kat returned to the table and gulped her coffee, wincing when the hot liquid stung her throat. "What else did you and Brody discuss?"

"He told me about Angel. That she died of pneumonia."

Kat was surprised Brody had confided in Ricky about his daughter. And why hadn't Brody mentioned the conversation to Kat? "When did you and Brody have this talk?"

"Last night." Ricky must have paid a visit to Brody when she'd been busy paying bills in her bedroom. No wonder Ricky had gone to bed earlier than usual—he'd been upset.

"What did Brody say—" *Don't.* "—when you asked him to marry me?"

"He said he couldn't raise another kid. I told him he didn't have to raise me, that you would, but I don't think Brody wants another family." Ricky's lips quivered and his eyes welled with tears.

Oh, honey, no…

"Brody's nice, Mom. I thought he liked us." Her son's voice cracked.

"Brody cares about us, but—" He's so sad inside that

he can't let himself be happy. "—rodeo is important to him, too."

Already in Ricky's short life four men had let him down. Dwayne barley acknowledged his responsibility to his son. Ricky's great-grandfather—the man who'd shown him the most love and affection had died. Then Seth had picked a job on an oil rig over her and Ricky. Now Brody, another man Ricky had grown to admire, chose to run from the demons chasing him rather than hold his ground and fight them. How much disappointment could a thirteen-year-old boy take before he became bitter and hardened inside?

"He'll come back after he's done riding bulls, won't he?"

"I don't know." Kat had her doubts that Brody would ever allow himself to accept forgiveness for the part he played in Angel's death.

Ricky wiped his damp cheeks. "Can we still live in Bandera, so I can go to the school in town?"

"Not if the Bakers don't want me to work for them."

"But you're good with the horses. And it wasn't your fault those guys quit. The Bakers should let you keep your job."

Kat smiled sadly. "Thanks for your vote of confidence, but too many things have gone wrong while the Bakers have been away."

"You mean the fire in the hay field and the horses getting loose?"

"Don't forget the debris jam in the stream."

"The Bakers can't blame you for that stuff."

"I was in charge, Ricky. I have to take responsibility

for what happened." A tough lesson both she and Ricky would have to learn from.

"If the Bakers are going to fire you, I bet it's because you're a girl."

"What are you talking about?"

"Stevie's mom says it's cool that you're a farrier, but she'd never want to do what you do, because men don't respect women for working a man's job."

Thank you, Stevie's mom. "There are a lot of ranchers who respect me, honey, but I admit that I have to work harder to prove I'm as qualified as a man to do my job. Just because things might not work out at the Wild Rose doesn't mean I'm throwing in the towel. Another opportunity for full-time work will come up."

"What are we gonna do until then?"

Her son knew darn well they'd have to go back to living on the move. Did he believe if he asked enough times her answer would change? Kat remained silent, hoping to avoid an argument.

"Whatever," he said. Although Ricky dropped the subject, Kat knew she hadn't heard the end of his pleas to remain in the area so he could attend school in Bandera.

"I need to fetch three yearlings from the pasture and shoe them today." She carried her empty coffee mug to the sink. "You can go to Stevie's after you muck the barn."

"Mom."

"What?"

"Would you let me live with Stevie and her parents? Her mom and dad like me a lot and they have an extra bedroom in their house. I could do chores for them to earn my keep."

Although she understood Ricky's feeling of helplessness over his situation, it hurt that he'd choose to live with his friend's parents and not her. "Let's take things one day at a time. Okay?"

Ricky didn't respond—not that she expected him to. "Catch you later." She left the cabin and hitched the horse trailer to the truck. Today her plan was to work herself to death. When she went to sleep tonight, she intended to be too exhausted to dream about Brody. To worry over his whereabouts... If he was alone...

If he was thinking of her.

Chapter Thirteen

"Look who finally came back." Riley Fitzgerald beamed at Brody.

Brody stood outside the men's restroom at the Palo Pinto County Livestock Association Rodeo Arena and Expo Center in Mineral Wells, Texas. He'd left the Wild Rose three days ago. Seventy-two hours of gut-wrenching misery. Misery loved company—but Brody wasn't in the mood to chitchat.

"Thought you'd come to your senses and retired from bull riding." Even though they competed in different events, Fitzgerald never missed an opportunity to encourage Brody to search for a new line of work.

Down in the dumps over leaving Kat and Ricky, Brody wasn't up for sparring with the cowboy. "Everyone knows I suck. What's your excuse for being here?"

Fitzgerald was one of the top saddle-bronc riders in the country. He'd won the NFR in Vegas last December when Drew had scratched his ride and handed the title to the black-haired Irish braggart. Since then the newspapers and reporters had had a field day dissecting Fitzgerald—half claimed he'd deserved the title, the other half claimed he didn't. Since the start of the season, Fitzgerald had yet to make the top five in the standings, which fueled more speculation that the title he'd won the previous year would be his last.

"What are you talking about?" Fitzgerald asked.

"If you're here instead of chasing the big money, that means you slipped out of the rankings."

The bronc rider's cheeks turned ruddy.

Brody could have taunted Fitzgerald, but he didn't have the energy. As a matter of fact, he didn't know where he'd find the strength to ride Nitro in less than an hour. "You get hurt?"

Something flashed in Fitzgerald's eyes then his shoulders slumped. "No."

"You draw a run of dinks?" On occasion a cowboy was assigned a horse with little bucking ability, which resulted in a low score even if the cowboy rode well and lasted eight seconds.

"Lost my timing is all." Fitzgerald straightened his posture. "I'll get it back."

The cowboy had better find his timing soon if he intended to make the finals in Vegas at the end of the year—not that the wealthy bronc rider needed the prize money. A cowboy's best chance for making money came during Cowboy Christmas, which lasted from January through July. Fitzgerald only had a couple of months to rack up his earnings and climb into the standings.

"I'm looking to get my timing back, too." Most cowboys broke out of their slump if they continued to compete. Not Brody. His slump was his average ride.

"Where'd you disappear to?" Fitzgerald asked.

No one except Drew Rawlins and now Katarina Sovo

knew about Brody's past. "Had to earn money for entry fees. I hired on at a ranch and mucked stalls. 'Course you wouldn't know much about having to work to pay your entry fees." Fitzgerald's father bred Kentucky Derby racehorses. The cowboy had a trust fund bigger than the state of Texas and a private jet at his disposal.

Ignoring Brody's jab, Fitzgerald changed the subject. "You hear from Rawlins much?"

"He's married now. Raises quarter horses on his ranch outside San Antonio."

"Did Rawlins ever say why he gave away the title to me?"

"Nope." Brody didn't discuss Drew's personal life with anyone. A man had a right to his privacy.

"Rawlins would have beaten me."

"I reckon he would have."

"Damn fans and the press won't cut me a break until I win another title."

"Fans can be finicky." Brody wasn't sure how he'd handle the intense pressure Fitzgerald was under.

"I've got a legitimate reason to ride, Murphy." Fitzgerald shook his head. "Damned if I can figure out why you're still competing. Every time you sit on a bull you put your life at risk."

"Doesn't matter if it's a bull or bronc, every rodeo cowboy risks his life when he competes in his event."

"Have you ever lasted eight seconds on a bull?"

"Nope. But there's always a first time."

"A first time for dying, too." Fitzgerald tipped his hat. "Don't get yourself killed today."

"As if you care whether I bite the dust or not!" Brody hollered at the bronc rider's retreating back.

Fitzgerald stopped and turned. "I may not care, but there must be someone somewhere who does."

There was one person who cared whether or not Brody lived to see another day. Kat. A glance at his watch confirmed that he had twenty minutes to prepare for his ride. No time to phone Kat—probably best. He wouldn't know what to say, even though he desperately wanted to hear her voice one more time…in case…He grabbed his gear bag and headed to the cowboy-ready area.

"Hey, Murphy! Where've you been?"

"Miss me, Jenkins?" Brody asked.

"He sure did," another of Brody's competitors said. "Now that Hollywood's back, Jenkins won't have to settle for last place." The bull riders chuckled.

"Guess you can't get enough of losing, eh, Murphy?" Buck Owens said.

Brody ignored the razzing, preferring to save his energy for his ride. He stopped next to chute five and introduced himself to Nitro. As far as bulls went Nitro was a handsome one—pure black with a white patch on his chest.

You going to play nice with me today, Nitro?

The bull stared straight through Brody. So much for trying to bond with the beast.

Brody dug out his bull rope and fiddled with it. His rodeo equipment was standard, nothing special. Nothing high-tech. He couldn't afford the newest gadgets and he doubted they'd help much anyway. A cowboy had to *want* to win or the best gear in the world wouldn't make a bit of difference.

Kat would be pissed if she knew what you're thinking.

Kat—sweet, pretty, determined Kat. She wanted to save Brody from himself, but the only person who could save Brody *was* himself. He thought of Ricky's father and how Dwayne had let Kat down by neglecting his responsibility to their son. If Brody had a son like Ricky he'd count his blessings and do everything in his power to be a good role model. Brody would teach the kid how to avoid the mistakes he'd made in life.

What kind of a role model do you think you are right now—risking your life when the odds are against you?

But Kat and Ricky aren't mine to care about.

They could be.

You ride bulls because you're looking for an out. A way to make the pain stop. The guilt to go away.

Kat's words echoed through Brody's mind. Until this moment he'd buried her harsh accusations deep in his subconscious.

Damn it, he wasn't trying to do what Kat had accused him of—he wasn't on a suicide mission. He pursued a rodeo career because it kept him on the move. Kept him busy. Kept him from having too much time to think. Kept his thoughts of Angel in check to a degree he could cope with. Why settle down in one place if he had no family? No one to come home to at night. No one to be accountable to.

Life on the move was best for him.

Kat calls it running.

Was he running? If so, where to? For how long? Until he got himself killed? Or so badly injured he could no longer climb on the back of a bull? The questions ricocheted off the inside of Brody's skull until a dull throb pulsed behind his eyeballs.

"Ladies and gentlemen, it's time for tonight's bull ridin' competition!" The announcer's voice startled Brody.

"We got ourselves eight eager cowboys ready to wrestle with eight ornery bulls." The crowd roared, but Brody ignored the noise, his focus on Nitro. For the life of him he couldn't come up with one damned piece of advice to offer himself. Unlike his competitors, Brody hadn't studied the art of the sport. He hadn't watched videotapes or taken notes on successful bull rides. And he usually disregarded free advice from his competitors because none of it mattered.

Then what's got you feeling different about this ride? Kat's insistence that Brody was trying to do himself in. Her belief that the only way he thought to snuff out the pain, guilt and sadness of Angel's death was to end his own life.

How the heck had Kat figured him out? Not even Drew knew Brody's greatest fear was living.

"We're startin' at the bottom of the barrel, folks. Brody Murphy's gonna give Nitro a run for his money. This cowboy's a character. He's got the worst record of any bull rider on the circuit and has never finished an eight-second ride. Don't know what keeps Murphy coming back for more punishment."

Something inside Brody shifted and a light switch went on. Suddenly he was tired of being the brunt of jokes. Yeah, he stunk at bull riding but he had his pride and he was determined that Nitro would not best him.

This one time, damn it, he wasn't going to go through the motions.

He was going to care about winning.

Care about his ride.

Care about his own ass.

He climbed the chute and swung a leg over the top rail. Nitro didn't twitch a muscle as Brody settled onto his back. That was more worrisome to a cowboy than a bull who thrashed in the chute. Sweat broke out across his brow and dripped down his temple as he positioned the bull rope and tweaked his grip. Never before had he perspired out of fear—exertion yes, but fear, no.

This is the ride of your life.

Heat radiated off the animal's back and Brody's inner thighs burned. A drop of sweat slid into the corner of his eye, blurring his vision. His heartbeat accelerated, which added to Brody's stress. The numbness that usually seeped into his brain and body was nowhere to be found.

Maybe he should have attended Cowboy Church with the other guys who'd gathered in an empty stock pen an hour ago. He wouldn't have said a prayer for himself, but he'd have asked God to keep Kat and Ricky safe. To make sure Kat got a permanent job at the Wild Rose. To see that Ricky enrolled in the junior high next fall. He would have asked Him to give Kat and Ricky a real home.

You think God would listen to a sinner like you? He nodded to shake off the voice in his head then signaled to the gate man that he was ready to ride. The chute door opened and Nitro bolted from his prison. Brody slid sideways, fear and sheer guts keeping his backside glued to the bull.

The stands blurred before Brody's eyes as images of Kat—smiling, laughing, frowning—filled his head. He saw her standing at the kitchen sink. Examining Tiger's hoof. Sitting behind the wheel of her truck. Facing off with Ricky over homework.

Wrapped in a bedsheet, her eyes begging him to stay.

A surge of adrenaline pumped through Brody, lending him the strength to hold on when Nitro spun viciously and followed the move with a buck that threatened to snap Brody's spine.

He never heard the buzzer—his mind was consumed with Kat—her scent, her big brown eyes, her smile... Time passed in a blur as Brody clung to the bull. Finally the bucking stopped and Nitro stood motionless in the middle of the arena. Silence echoed through the stands as the crowd came to their feet.

Brody blinked the images of Kat from his mind. Slowly he became aware of his surroundings and noticed the cowboys straddling the arena rails with their mouths hanging open.

Hot damn! He'd made it to eight. He leaped off Nitro and slapped the bull's rump, which sent the animal into a bucking frenzy. Brody made a dash for the rails amid thunderous applause.

"Well, folks. That was a first. In all my years announcin', I ain't never seen a cowboy ride a bull to a standstill. Looks like Brody Murphy not only lasted eight seconds, he's earned his highest score ever—a respectable ninety-one!"

After back-slapping and teasing from the other cowboys, Brody found his gear bag and stuffed his bull rope inside. He turned to leave and came face-to-face with Fitzgerald.

"Got to hand it to you, Hollywood, you sure do know how to put on a performance."

"You ride long enough you're bound to have good luck every now and then," Brody said.

Fitzgerald shook his head. "Luck had nothing to do with it. I think you finally found something worth riding for."

Maybe he had. Brody made a move past Fitzgerald, but the cowboy grabbed his shirtsleeve. "Aren't you staying to see if you win?"

"Nope. I'm going home." Tonight Brody had finally stopped running.

"NOT AGAIN," Brody mumbled out loud. Kat needed to invest in an ankle-monitoring bracelet for her son.

Brody honked, then swung his truck onto the shoulder of the road outside the Bandera town limits. Ricky kept walking. Brody honked again. The kid didn't even bother checking over his shoulder.

Shoving his head out the window Brody hollered, "Hey, Ricky! It's me, Brody!"

The teen stopped.

"You want a lift or what?"

Ricky's gaze connected with Brody's through the windshield. Slowly, one step at a time he backtracked to the truck. Brody lowered the passenger-side window. Ricky stared for the longest time then he raised his arm and wiped his eyes against his shirtsleeve.

Brody's gut twisted. "Hey, kid. You okay?"

Ricky didn't answer.

"C'mon. Get in."

Keeping his gaze averted, the kid hopped into the truck. Sweat dripped down his temples. Brody closed the windows and flipped the air conditioner to high. Aside from being hot, the teen appeared unharmed.

"I thought your mother told you not to thumb rides anymore."

"I wasn't hitchhiking. I was walking back to the ranch."

"You weren't looking for your dad again, were you?" A lengthy silence followed Brody's question.

"I was going to find you." Ricky's voice wavered.

Guilt slammed into Brody and he reprimanded the kid more harshly than he meant to. "You know better than to try to track down a man who's always on the move."

Finally Ricky looked him in the eye. "You left again without saying goodbye."

Brody considered mentioning his hurry to return to rodeo but that wasn't the real reason he'd left on the spur of the moment. Ricky's father had lied to the boy enough times already in his young life; Brody refused to do the same. "It was wrong of me to leave without telling you. I'm sorry." Ricky remained mute. "How are things at the Wild Rose? Clyde and Roger haven't given your mom any more trouble I hope."

"No. The Bakers are back."

"Did your mom get to keep her job?"

Ricky shrugged. "I don't know."

The tension in the truck was suffocating.

"Why are you here?" Ricky asked.

Because I'm tired of running, kid. "I need to speak to your mom."

"Brody?"

"What?"

"I know you miss Angel a lot, and you said you didn't want another family and—" Ricky sucked in a shuddering breath "—you don't want to be a father again, but if you stayed with me and Mom, you and I could just be friends. You wouldn't have to be like a stepdad or anything."

Brody's throat swelled and he couldn't speak. Several swallows later, he found his voice. "I guess you've been giving the three of us being together a lot of thought."

"Mom misses you."

"She said that?" Brody asked.

"No, but I can tell. She doesn't laugh as much. And late at night she's been sitting on the trailer steps by herself."

An image of Kat alone in the dark popped into Brody's mind and he hated that his actions had hurt her. That Kat missed him gave Brody hope she'd forgive him for being a coward.

Needing a moment to ponder how he intended to convince Kat he deserved a second chance, Brody asked, "You hungry?"

"Starving."

After checking traffic in both directions, Brody swung the truck around and drove into Bandera. He stopped at the Dairy Queen then handed Ricky a twenty-dollar bill. "Grab yourself a burger."

After Ricky entered the fast-food restaurant, a full-blown panic attack engulfed Brody. Sweat beaded his forehead and his palms became clammy. Now that he'd decided to face the past head-on he feared Kat would reject him. What in the hell would he do if she insisted on going it alone? How could he walk away from Ricky and Kat a third time when he yearned to be part of their lives?

Then fight for Kat.

Fight how?

Fight by staying. No matter where Kat went, Brody would follow. He'd sleep in his truck at night and find temporary work as a ranch hand by day. He'd show her that he was committed to her and Ricky.

A few minutes later Ricky returned to the truck. "I got you a burger, too."

Brody's queasy stomach rebelled but he appreciated Ricky's thoughtfulness. "Thanks, buddy."

Hoping conversation would take his mind off his worry whether or not Kat would allow him back into her and Ricky's life, Brody asked, "How are things between you and Stevie?"

"Good, I guess."

"I guess?"

Mouth full, Ricky said, "She wants to take it slow now, too."

Too?

"I asked her if she knew a lot about birth control and she kind of flipped out on me. So I said we didn't have to do anything and that maybe it was better if we didn't." Ricky shrugged. "Because what if we both liked someone different next year, you know? She agreed that we should just stay friends."

"Sounds like a smart plan."

"She said if I really wanted to kiss her I could sometimes."

Friends with benefits. "Kissing is okay, but it can lead to—"

"Yeah, I know. I told her I really wanted to stay friends because I liked fishing with her. And she said she wanted more riding lessons from Mom so we kind of struck up a bargain."

"Congratulations, Ricky." Brody grinned.

"For what?"

"For successfully negotiating the breakup of your first romance."

"Yeah, I guess you're right. We did break up."

"There will be lots of other girls but Stevie will always hold a special place in your heart when you think back on these years."

"I know. She was my first kiss and—" Ricky abruptly clamped his mouth shut.

"And what?"

Blushing, Ricky stared out the windshield. "She let me get to second base with her."

Brody pressed a napkin to his mouth to cover his smile.

"You know what?" Ricky asked.

"What?"

"Second base wasn't all that great."

"No?"

Ricky shook his head. "Stevie wears a padded bra and I didn't really get to feel her boob."

Brody busted up laughing. "Don't be in a hurry to grow up, kid."

"That's what Mom says." Ricky's expression grew thoughtful. "Mom had to grow up real fast because she got pregnant with me. I don't want to get some girl pregnant and cut out on her like my dad did to my mom."

"Anyone ever tell you that you're a decent young man, Ricky?" The kid grinned. Brody started the truck. "Let's get back to the ranch before your mother sends the sheriff after you."

"She won't. Mom thinks I went fishing with Stevie."

Chapter Fourteen

Where are you Brody?
What are you doing?
Do you miss me?

Thoughts of Brody were with Kat Monday afternoon as she changed the wrap on Tiger's hoof. Very little infection remained and she hoped this would be the gelding's final treatment. The Bakers had phoned the previous evening to inform Kat that they'd arrived at the ranch, but were too exhausted to meet with her. They planned to stop by the foreman's cabin today.

Kat wasn't looking forward to their chat, but she'd come to terms with her situation the past few days. She didn't deserve a permanent position at the Wild Rose. No matter that Clyde and Roger had caused a stink, a capable foreman would have been able to settle the dispute with the disgruntled employees and ensure the protection of the ranch and its livestock. Kat had failed to do that.

This morning she'd considered asking Ricky to pack his personal belongings but had chickened out when he'd begged to go fishing with Stevie. Kat hadn't had the heart to say no. She wanted her son to enjoy his last day at the Wild Rose.

Kat gave Tiger a final brushing, then murmured, "Be good for the Bakers, you hear?" Tiger whinnied. "If you don't screw things up the way I did, you'll have a nice home at the Wild Rose for the rest of your years."

The Bakers spared no expense in caring for their horses and Kat would miss working here. Better equipment made Kat's job easier and allowed her to keep more of her paycheck in her pocket. When she shoed horses on her own, she often used her money to purchase supplies that should have been provided by the owners. Sadly, some folks could barely feed their horses let alone pay for specialty items like soaking boots and the preemie diapers used to wrap hooves.

Kat led Tiger outside to the corral where a fresh bucket of oats awaited him. She spent the next hour cleaning the supply room and making a list of items the Bakers would need to stock up on soon.

Finished in the barn, Kat headed to the cabin for a quick shower. Aside from her and Ricky's clothes and a few personal items in the bedrooms and bathroom, most of the furnishings would remain in the cabin after they departed. A half hour later, dressed in clean clothes, she sat on the bed and held a photograph of Ricky. He looked more like Dwayne than her. One day soon Ricky would grow out of his awkward adolescent stage and be as handsome as his father.

Kat wandered into Ricky's bedroom and studied the movie posters on the walls. She remembered the day she'd taken him to the Wal-Mart in San Antonio to purchase the posters. He'd been so excited to have his own room and not have to sleep on the pullout bed in the trailer.

And now, because you couldn't handle Clyde and Roger, your son is going to lose all this.

Fighting tears, she spent the next hour cleaning out the fridge. By late afternoon she'd transferred most of their belongings to the trailer, which felt claustrophobic after living in a two-bedroom home. Needing a break before she resumed packing, Kat stretched out on the bed to rest her eyes for a few minutes.

Big mistake. The scent of Brody's body still clung to the sheets. The tears she'd refused to cry all day escaped her eyes and dripped onto the pillow case. As much as she wished to hold on to her job at the Wild Rose, it wouldn't mean anything without Brody by her side.

Stop feeling sorry for yourself. Somewhere out there is the perfect man for you.

Therein lay the crux of the problem. Kat didn't want a perfect man. She wanted Brody.

Fearing all she'd do is sob if she remained on the bed, Kat washed her face, then sorted through the items from the cabin. She dropped her keepsake box, the contents spilling onto the floor by the recliner. On hands and knees, she picked up the pieces—her grandmother's wedding ring. Her grandfather's watch. Her and Ricky's birth certificates. A pink rabbit's foot she'd won at the fair on her fifth birthday. A plastic heart bracelet Ricky had given her for Christmas several years ago. She patted the carpet beneath the chair, and her fingers bumped the edge of a paper—a photograph.

Angel. Poor Brody. He'd be a wreck when he discovered his daughter's photo was missing.

A beautiful little girl in a red cowboy hat sat perched on the top rung of a pasture fence. Her smile lit up her entire face as she hugged Brody's neck. Long blond curls blowing in the breeze, Angel looked like a feminine version of her father. Brody appeared happy, as if he hadn't a care in the world.

Kat considered Brody a handsome man, but he was drop-dead gorgeous in the photo. He looked ten years younger than he did now. Angel's death had taken not only an emotional toll on him but also a physical one.

The photo made everything real—Brody's pain, his suffering, his struggle to survive each day.

What do I do, Angel? I love your father, but he can't forgive himself for what happened to you.

Instead of the deceased child answering, Kat heard the sound of tires on gravel. She looked out the trailer window. The Bakers were here. Time to face the music. Kat left the trailer and met the couple in the middle of the ranch yard. She opened her mouth to greet them, but Melissa spoke first.

"Kat, I apologize for all the trouble Clyde and Roger gave you." The older woman shoved a hand through her gray, short-cropped hair. "I never expected the men to become jealous when Mark put you in charge."

"Before we left," Mark said, "I should have laid down the law with those two ignoramuses."

Kat didn't deserve the Baker's empathy. "You put me in charge and I failed to handle the situation." Kat stared at the ground then forced herself to meet Mark's gaze. "I selfishly wanted to make a good impression so you'd consider hiring me full-time. Because of that I refused to notify the sheriff when the trouble first began. If I'd reported the problem right away its possible Clyde and Roger wouldn't have taken their pranks as far as they did."

"I'm not sure I would have handled things differently in your shoes, Kat."

She appreciated Mark's understanding, but a few kind words didn't change the fact that she'd done a poor job keeping the ranch and the horses safe.

"I'm relieved you brought in Sheriff Conrad after Wes discovered the blockage in the stream," Mark said. "Melissa and I drove out to the pasture this morning to view the damage. We're going to press charges if the sheriff can prove Clyde and Roger were responsible for putting all those tree limbs in the water."

"I never thought the men would take things as far as they did just because I asked them to mow the hay. With rain in the forecast, I had to make sure the crop was safe in the barn."

"You made the right call about the hay." Mark's eyes shone with admiration. "And saved me thousands of dollars."

"Clyde and Roger insisted they were cowboys not farmers. I threatened to fire them and they walked off the job."

"I admit I'm stumped by their behavior. They've been with us several years and have never done anything this reprehensible." Mark swept his hands in front of him. "I'm impressed that you were able to bring in the hay and keep up with the horses."

Kat cleared her throat. "I didn't exactly bring in the hay."

Melissa quirked an eyebrow. "You hired another hand while we were gone?"

"Yes. Ricky ran into a rodeo cowboy at the festival in Bandera this past March. His name is Brody Murphy. Clyde and Roger had just quit, so I offered Brody the trailer and a weekly paycheck in exchange for harvesting the hay and mucking horse stalls."

"Where is this Brody Murphy? I'd like to meet the man," Mark said.

"He left after he cleaned up the stream. He wanted to get back to rodeoing."

"I wish things had gone differently while we were away," Mark said.

Kat winced but held her head high. She'd done the best she could under the circumstances. "I understand. I've got most of our things packed already. As soon as Ricky returns from fishing with a friend we'll clear out."

Melissa gasped. "You're leaving?"

Confused, Kat said, "After all that's happened, I assumed you wouldn't be offering me a permanent position."

"None of this was your fault, Kat," Mark said.

"We want you stay at the Wild Rose." Melissa glanced at her husband. "Shall I tell her?"

"Go ahead."

"We're expanding our horse operation to include

Andalusians," Melissa said. "We purchased two mares and a stud while in Spain and the horses will arrive next month."

Kat had heard of the pure Spanish horse but had never seen one in the flesh. Through the ages, Andalusians were recognized for their prowess as a war horse and their popularity with nobility. They were also known for their intelligence, sensitivity and docile manner. Today the breed was used in classical dressage events.

"The horses are extremely valuable, and we want only the best taking care of them," Mark said.

"Please say you'll take the job. You and Ricky can make the foreman's cabin your permanent home at the Wild Rose."

"I don't deserve the job," Kat felt compelled to say.

"Everyone deserves a second chance," Melissa said.

Kat waited for the euphoria to kick in. She and Ricky had a real home—a place to set down roots. Her son could attend school in the fall and participate in sports and clubs, while Kat earned a steady paycheck each month. Her dream had finally come true, but without Brody to share it, she couldn't muster any excitement. She shoved her hand in her back pocket and her fingers bumped the edge of Angel's photograph. She removed the picture.

"What do you have there?" Melissa held out her hand and Kat gave her the photo. "What a beautiful child. And such a handsome man."

"That's Brody. And his daughter, Angel. She died two years ago from pneumonia."

"I can see why you asked him to stay on, Kat." Melissa's eyes twinkled.

"Brody used to be a ranch hand in Montana before his daughter died. He and his wife divorced after Angel's death, then he joined the rodeo circuit and has been on the move ever since."

"Do you think Brody might consider becoming a permanent hand at the Wild Rose?" Mark asked.

Tears burned Kat's eyes and she bit her lower lip. If only a job stood in the way of her and Brody's happiness. "I don't know."

"Why don't you track Brody down and see if he'd like to work for us," Melissa said.

Why bother? Brody would snub the job. He wouldn't settle anywhere until he shook the demons riding his back. She hated to get the Baker's hopes up...hated to get her hopes up. "I'm not sure he's ready to quit rodeo." Kat ignored Melissa's sympathetic look. Had the older woman guessed that Brody had already broken Kat's heart?

"Tell you what," Mark said. "You find Brody and ask him to work at the Wild Rose for a while. If he likes taking orders from you and me, he's got the job for however long he wants. Otherwise he's free to move on, no hard feelings."

For the first time since Brody left, Kat felt a glimmer of hope. Brody was far from the ideal mate, but she and Ricky had their faults, too. Still, the three of them together were perfect. One way or another she'd find Brody and convince him to return to the ranch.

Right then a horn rent the air and they swung their

attention to the road. A red truck sped toward the barns, dust billowing in its wake.

Brody. You came back! "That's Brody."

Mark cleared his throat. "Melissa and I are heading up to the main house." He nodded to the red Dodge. "Let us know if he's interested in the job."

Kat managed a nod as the couple got into their sedan. Mark honked when he passed Brody's truck on the road. As the Dodge Ram drew closer, Kat recognized her son sitting in the front seat. *Not again, Ricky.* As soon as he got out of the truck, Kat issued a threat. "You better not have run off again, Ricky Sovo, or this time I am grounding you for life."

Her son had the audacity to grin at her. Kat switched her attention to Brody. They locked gazes, then the corner of Brody's mouth lifted in a smile, which sent Kat's pulse skyrocketing. Had he returned for Angel's photograph or did she dare hope he'd changed his mind about her…them?

Brody couldn't take his eyes off Kat. His memories of her didn't do justice to her earthy beauty. Ricky kept talking but he didn't hear a word the kid said, because all his senses were attuned to Kat. He rounded the hood of the truck, but stopped at the sober stare Kat sent him.

Did you assume you'd waltz back into Kat's life and she'd greet you with open arms?

Forcing one boot in front of the other, he crossed the drive until he stood in front of her.

"Kat."

"Brody." Her voice wavered.

The tension in the air was so thick he doubted a sledgehammer would crack it.

"Hey, Brody." Ricky poked his arm. "Look what you forgot." He pointed to the photo of Angel that Kat held in her hand.

Brody braced himself for the sharp piercing pain he always experienced when he stared at the picture of him and his daughter—taken four months before Angel had fallen ill. Kat handed him the photograph. A sadness filled Brody but the pain was nowhere near the agony he usually experienced.

"Ricky. Brody and I need to talk. Why don't you—"

"I know, get lost. But, Mom, I swear I just went into town to check if anyone had seen Brody. I was coming back."

"You told me you were going fishing with Stevie."

"I didn't want you to get your hopes up if I couldn't find Brody."

"We had a long talk, Kat, and Ricky won't be taking off anymore without telling you."

Ricky nodded. "I promise, Mom."

"I'm holding you to that promise, young man. Now go to the trailer and unpack our things."

Ricky frowned, then his eyes widened. "The Bakers let you keep your job?"

"Yes, they did." Kat's eyes watered. "You'll be going to school in Bandera this fall."

Ricky fist-pumped the air. "Cool!" He sprinted to the trailer.

"Congratulations, Kat." Panic swelled inside Brody. Ricky didn't need Brody to make it possible for him to attend school in town. Kat didn't need him to help her make ends meet. "I'm glad the Bakers realized what a great asset you are to their operation." An awkward silence settled between them and Brody felt his courage slip.

"Why did you come back?" Kat asked.

He took off his Stetson. "I'm tired of running."

Kat's eyes widened.

"I don't know where to begin."

Kat nodded toward the cabin porch and he followed her. They sat on the steps, Kat keeping two feet of space between them. He rubbed his brow then blew out a deep breath. "I've been on the run since Angel's death and not until you asked me to stay and help after Clyde and Roger left did I consider quitting rodeo. Living at the Wild Rose with you and Ricky went against everything I'd done in the past to survive." His mouth curved in a half smile. "You're the first person I've met who's made me want more from life."

"Then why did you leave?"

He searched for the right words to explain his jumbled thoughts. "Being with you loosened the tight band that's been squeezing my chest since Angel's death. For the first time in a long while, when I was around you I was able to breathe easier." He gazed into Kat's pretty brown eyes. "I felt safe with you even though I didn't deserve to feel that way." Kat's fingers slid through his and he tightened his grip on her hand, grateful for her compassion.

"I wanted to stay, but I was afraid of failing you and Ricky the way I'd failed Angel. I decided it was safer to keep my distance."

"Safer for whom?" Kat asked.

"Me." He cleared his throat. "I had to go back on the road because rodeo was the one thing I could do that wouldn't affect anyone but me. The only person who'd ever get hurt was me."

"And you didn't care if you got hurt."

"No. Until you accused me of being on a suicide mission, I hadn't wanted to believe that I was capable of such a deed, but it was true. Deep down I think I've been looking for a way to end the guilt and snuff out the pain." Brody shook his head. "After Angel died, I embarked on a course of self-destruction, because I believed I didn't deserve a second chance at happiness or even a second chance at being part of a family."

"Do you still believe you're unworthy of love, Brody?"

"No." He pressed a finger to Kat's mouth. "I'm a wreck on the inside. I'm not good enough for you and Ricky. But you made me realize that life is precious and I'd be a fool to waste the years I have left riding bulls."

Tears pooled in Kat's eyes and one escaped. Brody wiped the moisture with his thumb. "I'll go to my grave believing my selfishness played a part in my daughter's death, but if I can honor Angel's memory by not making the same mistake with you or Ricky, then maybe that's all I need to understand. I can't think of anything I want more than to put my bull riding days behind me and be a part of a family again."

Tears burned his eyes. "I realize we haven't known each other long, but—" he swallowed hard "—I love you, Kat." He tipped her chin and brushed his lips across her mouth in a fleeting kiss. "You can do a lot better than me, but if you give me half a chance I'll work hard to be a man you can depend on. A man who won't let you down. A man who'll support your goals and a man who'll try his damnedest to make your dreams come true." He brushed his lips across hers a second time. "And I promise I'll do everything in my power to never disappoint Ricky."

"What are you asking, Brody?" Kat whispered.

"I'm asking you to marry me, Kat. Make me whole again. Give me a reason to live. A reason to enjoy life. A reason to believe my daughter forgives me and wants me to be happy."

"Yes," Kat whispered. "Yes, I'll marry you."

Brody sealed his proposal with a kiss, then pulled back and frowned.

"What is it?"

He told himself it didn't matter. That he should be grateful Kat was giving him a chance, but… "Do you…I mean, do you think one day you might be able to—"

"I love you, Brody. I'm so sorry about Angel. If I had the power I'd bring her back to life for you, even if that meant we couldn't be together."

Brody believed Kat. Only a parent, driven by their love for a child would make such a sacrifice.

He pulled Kat close, soaking up her strength, her forgiveness, her love. "I've been thinking of employment options. I want to make sure I can help support you and Ricky and—"

"The Bakers are expanding their operation to include Spanish Andalusians and they need an extra hand to help train the horses."

Brody held his breath, afraid to hope.

"They offered the job to you, Brody. I told them I hired you and how you brought in the hay and helped clear the logjam in the stream. But there's a catch."

"What's that?"

Kat's lips quivered. "You'd have to take orders from a woman."

"I think I can handle that." Brody nodded over his shoulder. "And the cabin?"

"Is ours for however long we want to make our home here."

"How long do you want to stay?"

"Long enough for Ricky to graduate from high school. Then I don't care where we go."

"What about kids, Kat? I don't know if I've got it in me." The idea of being responsible for a tiny baby terrified Brody.

"We'll take it one day at a time. Right now I couldn't be any happier than I am. If you and Ricky and me is all we ever are, then I'm the luckiest woman in the world."

"I'm the fortunate one." Brody grabbed her hand and hauled her off the step. "Let's tell Ricky the good news."

"Wait." Kat tilted her mouth toward his. Brody didn't need any further prompting. Their kiss was warm, gentle and full of forgiveness and promise.

"Hey, does this mean Mom agreed to marry you, Brody?" Ricky yelled from the trailer steps.

Brody broke off the kiss. "I told Ricky when I spotted him hitchhiking back to the ranch that I was on my way here to ask you to marry me."

Eyes twinkling, Kat hollered, "Yes, I'm going to marry Brody!"

"Whoo-hoo!"

"I second that," Brody said, his mouth inching toward Kat's. "Whew-hoo."

* * * * *

Be sure to look for
Marin Thomas's next book in the
RODEO REBELS miniseries from
Harlequin American Romance!

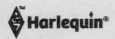
Harlequin®

American ★ Romance®

COMING NEXT MONTH

Available August 9, 2011

#1365 LAST CHANCE COWBOY
American Romance's Men of the West
Cathy McDavid

#1366 MY TRUE COWBOY
Men of Red River
Shelley Galloway

#1367 RANGER DADDY
Fatherhood
Rebecca Winters

#1368 A MOTHER'S HOMECOMING
Tanya Michaels

You can find more information on upcoming
Harlequin® titles, free excerpts and more at
www.HarlequinInsideRomance.com.

REQUEST YOUR FREE BOOKS!

2 FREE NOVELS PLUS 2 FREE GIFTS!

LOVE, HOME & HAPPINESS

YES! Please send me 2 FREE Harlequin® American Romance® novels and my 2 FREE gifts (gifts are worth about $10). After receiving them, if I don't wish to receive any more books, I can return the shipping statement marked "cancel." If I don't cancel, I will receive 4 brand-new novels every month and be billed just $4.49 per book in the U.S. or $5.24 per book in Canada. That's a saving of at least 14% off the cover price! It's quite a bargain! Shipping and handling is just 50¢ per book in the U.S. and 75¢ per book in Canada.* I understand that accepting the 2 free books and gifts places me under no obligation to buy anything. I can always return a shipment and cancel at any time. Even if I never buy another book, the two free books and gifts are mine to keep forever.

154/354 HDN FEP2

Name _____ (PLEASE PRINT) _____

Address _____ Apt. # _____

City _____ State/Prov. _____ Zip/Postal Code _____

Signature (if under 18, a parent or guardian must sign)

Mail to the **Reader Service:**
IN U.S.A.: P.O. Box 1867, Buffalo, NY 14240-1867
IN CANADA: P.O. Box 609, Fort Erie, Ontario L2A 5X3

Not valid for current subscribers to Harlequin American Romance books.

Want to try two free books from another line?
Call 1-800-873-8635 or visit www.ReaderService.com.

* Terms and prices subject to change without notice. Prices do not include applicable taxes. Sales tax applicable in N.Y. Canadian residents will be charged applicable taxes. Offer not valid in Quebec. This offer is limited to one order per household. All orders subject to credit approval. Credit or debit balances in a customer's account(s) may be offset by any other outstanding balance owed by or to the customer. Please allow 4 to 6 weeks for delivery. Offer available while quantities last.

Your Privacy—The Reader Service is committed to protecting your privacy. Our Privacy Policy is available online at www.ReaderService.com or upon request from the Reader Service.

We make a portion of our mailing list available to reputable third parties that offer products we believe may interest you. If you prefer that we not exchange your name with third parties, or if you wish to clarify or modify your communication preferences, please visit us at www.ReaderService.com/consumerschoice or write to us at Reader Service Preference Service, P.O. Box 9062, Buffalo, NY 14269. Include your complete name and address.

HAR11B

*Once bitten, twice shy. That's Gabby Wade's motto—
especially when it comes to Adamson men.
And the moment she meets Jon Adamson her theory
is confirmed. But with each encounter a little something
sparks between them, making her wonder if she's been
too hasty to dismiss this one!*

*Enjoy this sneak peek from ONE GOOD REASON
by Sarah Mayberry, available August 2011
from Harlequin® Superromance®.*

Gabby Wade's heartbeat thumped in her ears as she marched
to her office. She wanted to pretend it was because of her
brisk pace returning from the file room, but she wasn't that
good a liar.

Her heart was beating like a tom-tom because Jon Adamson had touched her. In a very male, very possessive way.
She could still feel the heat of his big hand burning through
the seat of her khakis as he'd steadied her on the ladder.

It had taken every ounce of self-control to tell him to
unhand her. What she'd really wanted was to grab him by
his shirt and, well, explore all those urges his touch had
instantly brought to life.

While she might not like him, she was wise enough to
understand that it wasn't always about liking the other person. Sometimes it was about pure animal attraction.

Refusing to think about it, she turned to work. When
she'd typed in the wrong figures three times, Gabby admitted she was too tired and too distracted. Time to call it a
day.

As she was leaving, she spied Jon at his workbench in
the shop. His head was propped on his hand as he studied
blueprints. It wasn't until she got closer that she saw his

eyes were shut.

He looked oddly boyish. There was something innocent and unguarded in his expression. She felt a weakening in her resistance to him.

"Jon." She put her hand on his shoulder, intending to shake him awake. Instead, it rested there like a caress.

His eyes snapped open.

"You were asleep."

"No, I was, uh, visualizing something on this design." He gestured to the blueprint in front of him then rubbed his eyes.

That gesture dealt a bigger blow to her resistance. She realized it wasn't only animal attraction pulling them together. She took a step backward as if to get away from the knowledge.

She cleared her throat. "I'm heading off now."

He gave her a smile, and she could see his exhaustion.

"Yeah, I should, too." He stood and stretched. The hem of his T-shirt rose as he arched his back and she caught a flash of hard male belly. She looked away, but it was too late. Her mind had committed the image to permanent memory.

And suddenly she knew, for good or bad, she'd never look at Jon the same way again.

Find out what happens next in ONE GOOD REASON, available August 2011 from Harlequin® Superromance®!

Celebrating
Blaze **10** years of
red-hot reads

Featuring a special August author lineup of
six fan-favorite authors who have written
for Blaze™ from the beginning!

The Original Sexy Six:

Vicki Lewis Thompson
Tori Carrington
Kimberly Raye
Debbi Rawlins
Julie Leto
Jo Leigh

Pick up all six Blaze™
Special Collectors' Edition titles!
August 2011

Plus visit
HarlequinInsideRomance.com
and click on the Series Excitement Tab
for exclusive Blaze™ 10th Anniversary content!